DIRTY OLD MANATEE

FREAKY FLORIDA BOOK 6

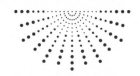

WARD PARKER

MAD MANGROVE MEDIA

1

BEACHED MALE

You have to be a night person when you're a nurse for vampires. There's no getting around it. Even though Missy Mindle also cared for werewolves, trolls, ogres, and other supernaturals through her home-health agency, the vampires' aversion to daylight determined her schedule.

Some folks have no problem working the graveyard shift. But all would admit that it messes with your social life.

Launching their kayaks from a sandy beach on Florida's Intracoastal Waterway, Missy and Matt were at the opposite ends of their day. Missy had worked all night giving health screenings to grumpy senior vampires. Saturday at 7:00 a.m. was Happy Hour for her. Her friend Matt Rosen was barely awake yet. With the circles under his bloodshot eyes, it appeared that he'd celebrated Happy Hour last night, and it hadn't ended early or well. He mumbled something about being out past midnight. Missy was smack in the middle of reading a vampire's blood pressure at midnight.

"Let's go north through the mangrove preserve," Missy said,

paddling away from the launch area. The waterway was very wide there, giving them plenty of room to explore far from the main boat channel.

"Have you ever considered not caring for vampires?" Matt asked, paddling just behind her. "Wouldn't you love having a normal schedule?"

A great blue heron squawked in annoyance at their approach and took flight.

"I'm the nurse they request the most from Acceptance Home Care. And I've become quite close to my vampires. They need me. And they're like grandparents to me. Grandparents who never die."

"Sharing the road around here with eighty-year-olds is pretty scary. With 800-year-olds, it's horrifying."

"Don't drive at night, then. And stay away from the Mega-Mart and the mall."

"Because it's not bargains they're hunting for. Have you ever considered caring for human patients again? You know, we humans aren't so bad."

Matt was one of the few humans who knew about the supernaturals living in Jellyfish Beach, Florida. He'd partnered with her many times to investigate mysteries involving monsters, and he had sworn to keep it all secret. The biggest threat to supernatural creatures was being exposed as real.

"Are you complaining because we don't go on dates?" Missy asked.

They both knew that Matt had a thing for Missy. She found him cute and endearing, maybe even sexy, but she was reluctant to possibly jeopardize their friendship by getting romantic. Besides, she was enjoying being single in midlife. She still had regrets after marrying a guy who left her for a gay vampire before being turned and, soon afterward, staked. There was no rush to blunder into more mistakes.

Therefore, Matt's and her relationship mostly consisted of getting together for breakfast or kayaking at the end of her day and the beginning of his. Sometimes, they would meet for dinner before she went to work, but she knew these dinners frustrated him because they wouldn't lead to anything afterwards. She had vampire urine samples to collect, after all.

She could feel Matt's eyes boring into the back of her head. He was pouting. Their morning meetings might lead to something on the days he wasn't working, but Missy had already made it clear she was exhausted today and needed to catch up on her sleep after their kayak trip.

Up ahead was another park. Unlike the one they had launched from, which was on the barrier island, across the street from the beach, this one was on the mainland. It had several acres of untouched mangroves growing out of the water, crisscrossed with tiny winding creeks.

Missy checked for oncoming boats, then raced across the channel near a red marker on a piling. Matt was right next to her, the spray from his paddle landing on her boat. He grinned at her.

She found an opening in the trees and drifted into it. These were red mangroves, perched atop their prop roots as if they were legs. With Matt behind her, she carefully steered her boat through the twisty stream, the water extremely shallow. She bent at the waist to avoid a low-hanging branch. Two yellow-crested night herons perched on a mangrove bough stared at her. Then they flapped their graceful wings and departed.

Up ahead, the creek widened and opened onto a small cove near land. That's when she saw the manatees. Two of them were in the shallows near the shore, their backs exposed.

"Matt, look," she whispered, pointing to the giant sea cows.

"Awesome," he said, snapping a picture with his phone.

She tried to get a little closer to the creatures, but not enough to scare them. She soon noticed something was wrong.

They lay on their sides, their whiskered snouts just breaking the surface of the water. They breathed with shuddering breaths.

Of the two, one was slightly larger. Both were mature and had the signs of many years in the water: bits of moss attached to their hides and propeller scars on their backs from careless boaters.

"Oh, my," she said. "I think they're ill."

She was no marine biologist, but knew that outbreaks of red tide or green algae sickened manatees. She was as close as she dared to get, and the creatures looked underweight.

"I'm calling Florida Fish and Wildlife," Missy said.

She called the FWC hotline, which she had memorized years ago after helping rescue a whale calf that had beached itself near Squid Tower where the vampires resided. After speaking with an operator, she was transferred to a local marine life rescue center. She gave them her GPS coordinates. Now there was nothing to do but wait.

She and Matt got out of their kayaks and pulled them onto the nearby bank.

"Manatees in estuaries are always in search of fresh water," she said. She picked up her water bottle and carefully approached the animals. She poured a trickle of water into the mouth of the smaller manatee. Its tongue moved, and it made swallowing movements, but the creature was mostly unresponsive.

Matt gave water to the larger one. It was more conscious than its companion. The manatee eagerly gulped the water, though much of it spilled from its mouth. Soon, the bottle was empty. Missy returned to her kayak to fetch another bottle.

While her back was turned, Matt made a high-pitched squeak.

"What. The. Heck," he said.

Missy turned. A naked man lay in the water in place of the larger manatee. Instead of two manatees, there was now one manatee and a fat, nude guy.

"What. The. Heck." Missy said.

The man was middle-aged, in his forties or fifties. He was fat and flabby. The front of his torso was mostly hairless and pale. Probably realizing his private parts were exposed, he rolled onto his stomach. His back was darkly tanned, with white slashes of scar tissue marking the same propeller wounds the manatee had. His head had human hair and a large bald spot.

The man propped himself up on his elbows to keep his head out of the water. Fatigue weighed down his body. He turned his face to them. He had a bristly goatee that matched the manatee's whiskers, bushy eyebrows, and a little piggy nose.

"Thanks for the water," he said. He had a gruff voice and the country accent of a farmer or cowboy.

"No problem, dude," Matt said. "Um, weren't you a manatee a few seconds ago?"

"Yeah. I didn't mean to shift in front of y'all. It's kind of embarrassing. But me and my old lady have been really sick."

"Old lady?" Missy asked.

"Yeah, her," the naked man said, nodding toward the manatee lying next to him. "That's my wife."

"Wife?" both Missy and Matt asked.

"Well, common-law wife, I guess. We're manatees. We don't have a marriage license."

"Please explain what's going on here so I don't check myself into a mental hospital," Matt said. "I was looking at two manatees lying in the shallows. Suddenly, one is gone and you're there instead."

"I thought it was obvious," the man said. "I'm a shifter. I can be a manatee or a human. For most of my life, I've been a manatee. I like that much better. I didn't intend to shift just now, but being sick and weak, I couldn't control myself."

"So you're a mermaid. I mean, merman," Matt said. "Or a mer-manatee?"

"A were-manatee?" Missy suggested. "Like a werewolf but a manatee instead?"

"I'm just Seymour. A guy who shifts between man and manatee."

"How?" Matt asked.

"I don't know. I concentrate really hard and envision the creature I want to be, and a strange feeling comes over me. Then it happens. I've had this ability most of my life. I only turn into a manatee. I tried to turn into a horse when I was a kid, but it didn't work. So, back to business, can you help my wife, here?"

"Of course," Missy said. "Sea Life Rescue Center is on its way. They have veterinarians and rehabilitation tanks. They can treat you, too, um, but not like this."

"Yeah, I know. Not as a human. I need to shift back to manatee."

"I'm a nurse and some of my patients are werewolves. Their body chemistry differs from normal humans', so they can't see doctors except for the most basic care. I wonder if that's the case with you."

"I don't know. I didn't go to the doctor much when I was

growing up as a human. My family was poor, and I ran away with the manatees when I was very young."

The rumbling of an approaching truck came from the park behind them.

"You need to put something on," Missy said.

"I have a rain suit," Matt said.

He opened a hatch in the bow of his kayak and pulled out a dry-bag. Inside were a rain jacket and pants. He was about to toss them to Seymour, but the naked man waved him off.

"Thanks," Seymour said. "But I don't want to be separated from my wife. Let me try to shift again."

He pushed himself away from the bank into slightly deeper water, closed his eyes and submerged his face. He lay unmoving, holding his breath far longer than Missy would ever be able to.

Nothing happened.

"That man is drowning," came a voice behind them.

A bearded guy wearing a Sea Life Rescue Center T-shirt stood there.

"No, he's okay," Missy said.

"He doesn't look okay to me."

"We'll take care of the man," Matt said. "You take care of the manatee."

"The call that came in said there were two of them."

"One of them got better."

The guy returned to his truck, and Seymour lifted his head from the water.

"I can't do it. I can't shift. Whatever illness we have is keeping me from shifting."

This time, he accepted the rain suit from Matt. Missy turned away while Seymour put on the pants and jacket.

The truck reversed to the bank with a beeping warning

signal. The vehicle looked like a flatbed tow truck. The bearded guy and a crew of two women and a man, wearing the rescue-center T-shirts, surrounded the female manatee and carefully rolled her onto a sledge of sorts covered with plastic. They attached a cable from a winch on the truck. The flatbed inclined and the winch slowly pulled the sledge from the water, up the bank, and onto the bed of the truck, which then returned to a horizontal position. The crew covered the sea cow with wet blankets and secured her with straps.

"Can we visit her to see how she's doing? Missy asked.

"Of course," one of the women said before getting into the rear seat of the cab. "We're open to the public on most days."

Missy thanked them and watched the truck drive away.

"What am I going to do now?" Seymour asked.

"Unless you get really sick, I wouldn't recommend going to the hospital. You're coming with me. I'm licensed to care for supernaturals. I'll try to get you well."

"Are you crazy?" Matt asked. "You just met this man. You're bringing him to your house?"

"He's a manatee-man. And he'll be just fine."

Matt pulled her aside. "What if he forces himself on you?" he whispered.

"He's married. Well, in an animal sense."

"Oh, yeah, like that ever stopped a man from trying to get some."

"Matt, he's in love with a manatee. He's not into human chicks."

"Don't be so sure about that," Matt said, sullen.

8

THEY HAD two one-person kayaks and three people. Whether you considered Seymour a full-fledged human, he was as large or larger than one, and he couldn't share a kayak with Missy or Matt.

"I'll swim along with y'all," he said.

"You're in human form now," Missy reminded him.

"I'm a great swimmer in either form."

But as they paddled toward the launch site, he had problems keeping up. He didn't do the Australian Crawl or the breaststroke. He attempted to mimic a manatee's tail-propelled swimming technique. It didn't work so well. He was also weakened by whatever illness afflicted him and his mate.

Matt paddled back to the launch on his own, promising to return with his truck. Missy brought Seymour, clinging to the stern of her kayak, back to the park where they had found him and waited for Matt.

Seymour sat on a grassy area just beyond the mangroves and rested his head on his hands. Matt's tan rain suit was much too tight for the shifter. His belly roll protruded, as the jacket couldn't close at the bottom. His butt crack was visible above the pants, which looked like they would split at any moment.

"I hope she's okay," he said. "We've never been separated before. That shows you how special our relationship is, because manatees don't normally form bonded pairs."

"We'll go to the rescue center and you can see her. What is her name?"

"She doesn't have a human name, of course. I call her Lubblubb, but it sounds different when I said it now than it does underwater in manatee language."

He rubbed the bristles on his face and bald head in worry and exhaustion. Missy felt sorry for the shifter, who was clearly more manatee than human.

"Are you hungry?" Missy asked. "I have energy bars."

"I'd prefer sea grass."

"Sorry, I'm fresh out. But, you know, in human form you probably need to alter your diet."

"I guess."

"When was the last time you were in human form?"

"I don't know. It's been years."

"I'm surprised it hasn't affected your ability to speak."

"Me too. I always felt humans talked too much. Like my mother. And my teachers. Manatees can express all there needs to be said with touch and gestures. Sometimes simple squeaks and chirps."

Matt arrived in his pickup truck, his kayak strapped to the bed. His facial expressions made it clear that he was not enjoying any of this. He handed Seymour an old pair of flip-flops so he wouldn't be barefoot. After he helped Missy load her kayak, she and Seymour slid onto the bench seat in the cab. Because of Seymour's size, Missy was pressed thigh-to-thigh with Matt. She rather liked the feeling. Matt's mood instantly perked up.

They drove the short distance to the Sea Life Rescue Center, a non-profit on Highway A1A, the two-lane beach road. It was on the west side, with a frontage on the Intracoastal. Inside, the rehabilitation tanks were open to the public. They walked past green and leatherback turtles paddling about. A larger tank in the rear was occupied by a manatee and her calf, but not Lubblubb.

Missy asked the elderly woman volunteer at the front desk where the new manatee was kept.

"If she's ill or injured, she'll be in the clinic in the back. But the pubic isn't allowed in there."

"One of her friends wants to see her."

"Friends?"

"I'm her mate," Seymour said. "I have a right to see her."

Missy elbowed him in his generous belly. "This gentleman means he is very familiar with this manatee. She comes to his dock regularly."

"I'm impressed you can tell what gender it is," the volunteer said, picking up the phone. "Let me ask the vet if she'll make an exception."

A tall, young black woman came out and smiled at them. "Are you the ones who found her?"

"Yes," Missy said. "We called you guys right away."

"Can I see her?" Seymour asked.

"Okay, but only briefly," the veterinarian said. "She's had too much stress and needs to adapt to her new surroundings."

"She's my mate," Seymour said.

Missy elbowed him in the stomach again.

"He means she's his spirit animal. She visits his dock every day."

The vet led them into a large room that was part laboratory and part clinic with two surgical tables. One tank held a hawks-bill turtle missing a flipper. In the other was Lubblubb. She floated listlessly, occasionally rising to push her whiskered nostrils above the surface for air.

Seymour rushed to the tank, pressing his face and hands against it. He cried softly.

"He's very sensitive," Missy explained to the vet.

When Seymour began utter high-pitched chirps and whis-tles, the vet's expression changed from pitying to puzzled.

Lubblubb touched her nose to the glass by Seymour's face.

Missy smiled as if this was all normal.

"Um, people rarely bond like this with manatees," the vet said. "Except perhaps workers at an aquarium."

"Or extremely deranged humans," Matt said.

Watching this interspecies show of affection was getting awkward for Missy. Especially with the glass of the tank all smeared with Seymour's snot and tears.

"Maybe we should go now," she said.

Seymour sobbed.

"She needs to relax," the vet said.

Finally, Seymour nodded and backed away from the tank. The vet patted him on the shoulder.

"We'll give her the very best care," she said.

As Matt ushered Seymour from the room, Missy asked the vet if she had any thoughts about what made the manatee sick.

"I truly don't know. There have been no reports of red tide in the area. I took blood samples and we'll see what the results tell us. We'll also test the water where you found her."

Missy thanked her and Matt drove them to Missy's car, still parked at the kayak launch site.

"So," Matt asked, "what are you guys going to do?"

"I'm taking Seymour home, setting him up in the guest room, then going to sleep. I've been awake since sunset Friday."

"Okay. Are you sure that's . . . safe?"

Was he implying that the guy he just saw blubbering and squeaking was a potential threat?

"We'll be fine," Missy said. "Thanks for the ride."

She loaded her kayak onto the rack atop her car and strapped it down. Seymour stood awkwardly nearby.

Matt's truck hadn't left yet.

"Are you going to be okay?" Matt asked.

"We'll be fine."

"I meant you."

"I'll be fine. I'll be sleeping."

"I'll call to check on you."

"I won't answer. I'll be asleep."

He finally got the point, waved weakly, and drove off. Meanwhile, Seymour continued to stand there uncomfortably.

"Get in the car, Seymour. I'll stop at Mega-Mart and buy you some clothes that will fit. Then we'll go home."

"Home is where the herd is."

"Not for now, Seymour. Not until you're feeling better and can shift back to manatee."

He got into the passenger seat and looked ahead dejectedly. His situation appeared to be sinking in.

"Seatbelt," Missy said as she started the engine.

She told Seymour to wait in the car when she arrived at Mega-Mart. She hurried inside and picked up some XXL underwear, sweatpants, and T-shirts, along with a pair of sandals. He also needed toiletry items. What else would a former manatee need? Of course, cheap sunglasses and a Miami Dolphins cap.

When they entered the house, Missy's gray tabbies, Brenda and Bubba, raced out to meet them. This was not normal behavior. Usually a visitor caused them to hide under the bed until they determined the person wasn't a psycho cat killer. Then, they would timidly venture forth to make introductions.

Today, the cats must have smelled something different about Seymour. That he was not one hundred percent human. Missy knew for a fact they had never met a manatee before and as far as she knew, cats and manatees didn't have a special affinity. They ran right up to Seymour, sniffed him, then rubbed against his legs. Missy was half tempted to call Matt and announce that her cats deemed Seymour to be non-threatening.

"I never had a cat," Seymour said. "Or a dog. My parents didn't allow me to have a pet. Maybe that's why I spent so much time at the river watching for manatees."

Missy wanted to hear his personal story, but with her vampire hours it was too late. The sun was high, and she'd been awake too long.

"Seymour, I'll make you a salad, and then I need to go to sleep."

He followed her into the kitchen.

"First, let me check your vital signs and take a blood sample."

She removed gear from the tote bag she brought on her home-health visits. First, she stuck a thermometer in his mouth.

"Don't chew that," she said.

She placed an oxygen clip on his finger and wrapped a blood-pressure cuff around his arm. His temperature and oxygen level were normal, though his blood pressure was slightly elevated. Maybe it was because he was overweight, though in manatee form he'd probably be fine.

She sat him down at the table and retrieved her blood kit from the tote bag. After she rubbed his arm with alcohol, he drew back in fear at the sight of the needle.

"Don't worry. It won't hurt. Close your eyes and this will just take a few seconds."

She filled two vials which she would send to the lab contracted by her employer to do testing of samples from her supernatural patients of all varieties. This lab tested even her werewolf and other shifter patients. Though they may seem perfectly normal when in human form, shifters had unique antibodies, antigens, and proteins in their blood that would cause a lot of consternation if a conventional lab discovered them.

She labeled the tubes, packaged them, and placed them in the metal box outside the front door where the samples from her vampire patients last night awaited pickup. Next, she washed and disinfected her hands so she could make Seymour a salad.

With Seymour observing, she took a tomato from a basket on the counter and placed it on the cutting board. Then she rummaged in the fridge, putting a head of iceberg lettuce on the counter, followed by romaine. She found a carrot and half an onion, but doubted a mer-manatee would like onion. She turned to place the carrot on the cutting board.

Both heads of lettuce and the tomato were gone. Seymour chewed, a frond of romaine protruding from his mouth.

"Yummy," he said.

"Okay. I guess I'm done here. Are you still hungry?"

"No, thanks. I feel a little ill and weak."

"You should get some rest now. You've had a traumatic day."

"Do you have a swimming pool where I can sleep?"

"No. And this human body of yours doesn't have natural buoyancy. You're going to sleep in a bed."

She led him to the guest bedroom with its queen-sized bed. It looked small for a big guy like him.

"It's been years and years since I slept in a bed," he said, looking at it dubiously.

"The bathroom's next door. You do remember how to use it, right? You can't just let loose whenever you want, like you're in the lagoon."

He acted insulted. "We do not 'let loose whenever we want.' We make sure we're downstream from the rest of the herd."

"That's good to know. There's a fresh toothbrush and tooth-paste in there, if you remember how to use them. Meanwhile, I'll say goodnight. Or good-day. If you get hungry, you can graze on whatever looks good in the kitchen."

Missy went into the master suite on the other end of the

hall. After making sure the cats were inside, she locked the door. Just in case.

She slept heavily, well past sunset.

NOT LONG AFTER the sunlight ebbed, a visitor appeared in Missy's backyard. It was a young Latinx woman, with closely cropped hair, studs in her nose and lower lip, and lots of ink. She was pale, haggard, and hungry.

She was a vampire. And she had a score to settle with Missy.

She approached the end of the house and stood outside the master bedroom windows. Her nostrils flared, and she sampled the air. She picked up the scent of the witch still sleeping inside. But there was another human, too. Not a normal human; there was something off about the scent. It was a male, perhaps a lover. His presence made preying upon the witch problematic.

Maria was a new vampire, turned only months before. She was unskilled at hunting, mesmerizing prey, and avoiding detection. That was because the vampire who had turned her was dead. Mona, her maker, should have been there to teach Maria all she needed to know to get by as a vampire in the world. It took cunning and skill to make it in a crowded place like South Florida. At first glance, it was teeming with prey, but all those humans meant more risk of being detected.

In a modern society that didn't believe in supernatural creatures, being detected was an existential danger. There were very few humans who knew that supernaturals existed. Among them was a small number of cops and others who wished to keep the peace by eliminating these creatures that most people believed did not exist.

A vampire who was found out often ended up staked to

death, extrajudicially executed on the spot. Experienced vampires knew how to keep that risk low. Maria did not. Her maker died before she could teach her how.

Her maker had been killed by Missy Mindle. Mona, Thogg, and others of her ancient clan, had taken over a community of vampire seniors, intent on conquering all the vampires in Florida and, then, the nation.

But this witch's magic had stopped them, destroyed them.

Mona was dead. And Maria was left to fend for herself, a homeless vagrant, sleeping during the day in sheds and beneath porches, forced to prey upon possums and rats. Maybe the occasional dog. Not yet upon the sweet blood of a human.

She lacked the skill to hunt, isolate, and mesmerize a human in order to drink his or her blood. Because she had no one to teach her.

Thanks to Missy Mindle.

Maria was determined that the witch would be her first human victim. And she would not simply drink her fill and leave her victim with no memory of what had happened.

No, she would drain the witch to the last drop. Until the witch was dead.

Maria stood outside the house for hours as the night progressed. When lights appeared in the bedroom windows, she lost her nerve.

She would return another time. Maybe by then, the other human would be gone.

2

TURN FOR THE WORSE

Missy rose from bed at 9:30 p.m., which was late for vampire hours. Yesterday and this morning had exhausted her. The first vampire patient scheduled tonight was at 11:00 p.m. at Squid Tower on the beach, so she was okay with time. Her inner clock would be challenged again in the morning, as she would have to kill time between her last appointment before dawn and a 7:00 a.m. screening with a werewolf patient in neighboring Seaweed Manor.

After she showered and dressed, she went to check on Seymour. His bed was empty. She took a quick tour of the house and didn't find him anywhere. Hopefully, he hadn't wandered off into the neighborhood.

A bubbling sound came from the guest bathroom, the only place she hadn't checked because the light was off and door ajar.

Seymour slept in the bathtub full of water, his head resting on the end of the tub with his nose just out of the water. He was, unfortunately, naked. Missy turned away from the jarring sight of man-boobs. As long as he didn't drown, he was welcome to sleep where he felt most comfortable.

Before she left the house, she began writing a note to tell Seymour where she kept various foods, but realized he might not know how to read. So she put apples and carrots in a visible place on the counter, along with cereal and bottles of water. After she fed the cats, whose diet was so much easier to understand, she grabbed her medical tote bag, double-checked that she was wearing her anti-vampire amulet necklace, and left for work.

Agnes Geberich, president of the Squid Tower HOA, was her first patient. She was in good health for a vampire whose body age was in its early nineties, meaning that's how old she was when she was turned into a vampire. The transformation took place over 1,500 years ago when she was a Visigoth noblewoman. Nowadays, the petite vampire's primary health complaints were a weakness in her legs and constipation. For vampires, constipation meant over three months since their last bowel movement.

"Bone marrow," Missy told her patient. "It's the only thing that vampires can digest that gets things moving down there."

"I've also been under a lot of stress lately," Agnes said. "That cannot but make things worse."

"Why? What's going on?"

"Ever since the Neanderthal vampires tried to subjugate the vampires in Jellyfish Beach, I've been working to unite all of us in Crab County, so we don't get caught as weak and unprepared as we were. I've found it quite difficult. It turns out vampires don't like to be united."

"How many vampires are there in the county?"

"That's the problem. I don't know. I doubt we'll ever know. The only place we're organized is here at Squid Tower and at

Alligator Hammock, another fifty-five-plus community west of town. The rest of the vampires in the area are younger in body age and live alone or in small hives. Many have night-shift jobs or work remotely and pass themselves off as humans. On the other hand, there are also criminal gangs of vampires."

"Yeah, I doubt they'll want to unite with you."

"I don't wish to establish a formal confederation. I simply want to know who is out there and how to get in touch with them if vampires are ever in danger again."

"How on earth do you find all these vampires?"

"The only way is to canvas the entire area street by street. I travel with Bill, Oleg and others who fancy themselves as geriatric tough guys. It's difficult for you to understand, but vampires have a sixth sense for identifying other supernaturals like ourselves. Often, we can sense that a home or building has vampires in it. Then there's nothing else we can do but ring the doorbell and introduce ourselves. It's like volunteering for a political campaign. Or being a Jehovah's Witness."

"Agnes, that sounds like it could be dangerous."

"Perhaps. But so far, my tough guys have discouraged anyone from attacking us."

"You know, it's probably a good idea to make inroads with other supernatural creatures, not just vampires," Missy said. "Like you have with the werewolves next door. It could be helpful in case humans come after you."

"I suppose you're right. But I don't foresee that happening on a grand scale. You see how many spats we get in with the werewolves."

"But a lot of that is petty stuff, like the werewolves leaving their dogs' poop on Squid Tower property."

"Missy, as a human, you don't understand what it's like to be a monster in this day and age. It's very polarizing. The ogres don't like the trolls. The Caribbean monsters don't get along with the European monsters. The Native American monsters don't like any of us. It's complicated."

"Well, I wish you luck with the vampires. And stay safe."

As Missy's workday stretched into daylight hours, it was time to visit her werewolf patients next door. Werewolves don't live forever like vampires, and when they retire and move to Florida, they treat their golden years like one never-ending party filled with carousing and howling at the moon. Even at 7:30 a.m., Missy smelled pot smoke in the breezeways.

Harry Roarke was eager for his physical to end so he could go surfing. But Missy kept peppering him with questions unrelated to his health.

"Do you know much about shifters other than werewolves?"

"Why do you ask?"

"I'm helping a shifter who spent most of his life as a manatee. He and his mate got sick, and now he's stuck in human form. And not happy about it."

"There are so many kinds of shifters and they're all different," Harry said. "Even among werewolves. Some became werewolves because of a magic curse. Others were born with the gene. But most of us are normal humans who were bitten by a werewolf and infected with a virus that caused physiological changes making us shift to wolf form. Since I doubt your friend was bitten by a manatee, he was probably born with a shifter gene."

"But why did it cause him to shift to a manatee?"

"The shifter gene isn't species-specific," Harry explained. "The first time in their lives that they shift, it will be to a creature they admire and empathize with. From then on, that's the only thing they'll shift into. There are exceptions. A woman who lives here can shift into almost any creature she wants, but that ability is very, very rare."

"What can hamper your ability to do it?" Missy asked.

"I've never had that problem. I'm a virile guy."

"I'm talking about your ability to shift."

"Yeah, of course. As a werewolf, nothing can keep you from shifting on a full moon. But if you want to shift at your own discretion, and you're really sick and weak, you might not be able to do it."

"Okay." That fit her theory of why Seymour was trapped in human form.

"I've also heard that magic can get in the way, too. I would have thought you knew that."

"It's not the kind of magic I know."

WHEN MISSY GOT out of her car in her driveway, she noticed the footprints. Big, wet, sloppy prints leading from the street, up the driveway, and along the concrete walkway to the front porch. She didn't have to guess who left them.

They continued through her foyer and into the living room. She grabbed a towel from the linen closet to clean the prints before the water damaged the hardwood floors. She followed them to her kitchen.

Seymour sat on the tile floor, leaning against the island. He was surrounded by a huge pile of wet water hyacinths. He stripped them of their leaves and flowers which he popped into his mouth.

"You went into the canal across the street for those?" Missy asked.

He nodded while munching the plants. He had trespassed through a neighbor's yard to reach the water, but she didn't bother saying it. The bigger offense was the fact that he was naked. Trespassing is one thing. Doing it while naked and flabby raises it to a whole new level of lawbreaking.

"You're going to need to try some alternate foods. The human body has different nutritional requirements than the manatee."

"This suits me just fine," he said through a full mouth. "You want some?"

"I could use some more fiber, but I think I'll pass."

"I want to see Lubblubb. Can you take me?"

"Yes, but only if you put some clothes on."

"Oh, yeah. Sorry. Clothing seems like such a strange concept."

"Welcome to Human World."

"I don't like it very much," he said.

When the volunteer saw them enter the rehabilitation center, she quickly spoke into her phone. Her expression alarmed Missy. The veterinarian came flying out of the back room.

"I'm so sorry," she said. "The manatee you helped rescue has died."

Missy felt grief for the creature she hadn't known. Seymour's face turned as white as a vampire's.

"What?" he asked in a quavering voice.

"She passed away from whatever illness she had," the vet said. "Again, I'm sorry."

Seymour buried his face in his hands, his body spasming with sobs.

"I've never seen anyone as attached to a manatee," the vet whispered to Missy.

"Can I see her?" Seymour asked as tears streamed down his face.

"No, I'm sorry. We performed a necropsy on her."

"Come, Seymour, sit down for a moment," Missy said. She led him to a bench along the wall.

Then she returned to the vet and asked about the blood test results.

"The tests came up negative for the usual suspects, including red tide. The water tested fine, too, but we sampled the area where she was found. Perhaps she ingested a toxin in a distant location. Based on the necropsy, I don't see signs of any common illnesses. Frankly, she looked like she had been poisoned with insecticide; but, again, we didn't find any traces of it. I'm sorry that I don't have anything conclusive to tell you."

Missy thanked her and sat next to Seymour. She gave him a hug. What do you say to someone who lost his soulmate? Also, there are few animals as gentle and endearing as a manatee. She felt so bad for Seymour.

His sagging jowls with sparse whiskers, his rounded nose, his droopy eyes—they all gave him that adorable manatee look. Missy couldn't keep herself from crying, too.

Once they were home, Seymour retreated to the guest bathroom to soak in the tub. His sobbing echoed throughout the entire house, so much that both cats went to investigate the source of the noise. They stayed in the bathroom, evidently to comfort the strange human with the animal scent.

Missy called Matt and told him the sad news.

"I searched our news archives, and I kept coming up with more deaths like this," he said. "No massive die-offs that would get a lot of attention, but lots of small groups of manatees beaching themselves and dying. All over the state. Both in fresh and brackish waters."

"Has anyone speculated on the cause?"

"Of course. We journalists depend on quotes from experts who speculate. But the causes they suggest are all over the board. Hypothermia for the deaths that occur during cold weather and a vast assortment of toxins for deaths the rest of the year. Or malnutrition. But there is definitely a worrisome trend. Lots of manatees are dying in Florida, more than those that get killed by boats each year."

"I want to look into this," Missy said. "I have a heartbroken man crying in the bathtub and I want to find out why he lost his mate. And why it's happening to other manatees."

"He's in your bathtub?"

"The guest bath. He likes to be immersed in water. Too bad I don't have a pool."

"Yes. Too bad."

"So how do we go about investigating this?"

"Why does it have to be 'we'?"

"C'mon, Matt. I need your help. You're a brilliant reporter. And you've helped me out so much in the past. We work great as a team, right?"

"Yes, we do make a good team," he said ruefully.

RICK HAZEN HAD BEEN a law enforcement officer with the Florida Fish and Wildlife Conservation Commission for thirty years. He was ready to retire. But the increasing number of manatees dying each month bothered him too much to walk away. There was something suspicious about the deaths. He suspected illegal dumping of pollutants was to blame, but he hadn't yet seen any water quality reports that backed up his hunch.

Still, when he patrolled the waters by boat, he was extra vigilant, always on the lookout for illegal dumping.

It was 3:00 a.m., near the end of his shift. This was when he often nailed illegal long-netters catching redfish and sea trout. He ran north on the Intracoastal at idle speed, navigation lights off. There was no boat traffic at this hour, so having his lights off wasn't dangerous. It did, however, allow him to sneak up to boats dropping nets.

He rounded a mangrove point, and there she was: a large go-fast boat built for racing, anchored outside of the channel. Not the kind of boat you'd expect to see at this hour.

Drifting silently toward it, he put on his infrared night-vision goggles. Men were moving about on the boat. They lifted a large drum and poured its contents into the water, putting the empty in the boat's stern. Now they were lifting a second drum.

He turned on the searchlight and blasted the men with its beam. They tried to see who he was, but continued to empty the barrel.

"F-W-C," he said into the loudspeaker. "Put down that drum and keep your hands in the air."

He got on the radio to HQ.

"This is patrol boat 539, approaching suspicious vessel in the Intracoastal Waterway in Jellyfish Beach north of Green Marker 42."

"Copy that. What's the violation?"

"Manatee Sanctuary Act," Hazen replied. "I think they're dumping toxins in the water."

As far as manatees were concerned, Hazen's job was to stop speeders in manatee zones, boats destroying sea grass in shallow waters, and the harassment of manatees. Polluting was

up to the Department of Environmental Protection to prose-
cute. But he could report the violation to them.

He drifted closer to the boat in order to see the registration
number on the hull.

"Registration is FL 3712 WZ."

"Copy that."

"I'm going to board the vessel."

He was close to the other boat now. The three men stood
watching him, their hands only half-heartedly raised just above
their waists. They wore shorts and fishing shirts, nothing out of
the ordinary. One of them was quite tall with long, blond hair,
and held himself with the bearing of being their leader.

Hazen kicked over the two fenders tied to his boat so he
could drift into the suspects' vessel without damage.

"What are you gentlemen dumping into the water?"

"Beer," said the tall one. His long blond hair was like a rock
star's.

"Why in the world are you dumping beer into the Intracoastal"

"We're coming home from a party and wanted to get rid of it
before we got to the boat ramp," the man said. His accent
sounded Russian. "It's that pumpkin-spice ale. I can't stand it,
personally."

Hazen could understand trying to hide the evidence to
avoid a boating under the influence charge. But three big
barrels filled with beer? And since when did beer come in
barrels instead of kegs?

"I'm coming aboard to inspect your alleged beer," Hazen
said. "Florida doesn't take kindly to polluters of our
waterways."

The tall man laughed. "I agree that pumpkin-spice beer
should be classified as a pollutant."

Hazen stepped onto his gunnel to climb onto the taller vessel.

"But I don't give you permission to board," the tall man said.

The man reached into his shorts and pulled out a large handgun. The barrel was only two feet from Hazen's face when it fired.

MATT'S POLICE radio scanner came alive shortly after 3:00 a.m. and woke him from a deep sleep. It was tuned to the frequency of the Jellyfish Beach Police Department, which meant it was usually silent. There wasn't much crime in the city. Matt regretted that, because as a general assignment reporter, he found writing articles about crime much more interesting than covering city government or county commission meetings.

On any given weekend, there might be a call coming over the scanner about seniors coming to blows at Bingo Night, or a simple shoplifting call or two. At least once a week there would be a call about a naked Florida Man, drunk or on drugs, or both, committing petty crime or disrupting traffic.

However, this call was different. This dispatcher, anguish in her voice, reported the shooting of a Florida Fish and Wildlife Conservation Commission officer. This was serious and disturbing, completely unlike Jellyfish Beach.

Matt dressed and drove to the park on the Intracoastal where the public boat ramp was located. Paramedics lifted a stretcher from a Crab County Fire Rescue boat at the dock and wheeled it to a waiting ambulance. A uniformed police sergeant blocked Matt from getting any closer. It was Tim Feldman, a former high school classmate of Matt's.

"Rosen, you must still be using your scanner. Your showing up is more dependable than mail delivery."

"Hey, Tim, can you tell me anything? Did he or she survive?"

"He was an officer from F-W-C. And no, he didn't make it. He was shot point-blank in the head when he tried to board a boat suspected of dumping toxins or something."

Manatees was the first thing that popped into Matt's head. Were the bad guys the ones dumping whatever substance killed Lubblubb?

"Who reported the shooting?" Matt asked.

"F-W-C, after they lost contact with the officer. He called in a registration number, which turned out to be a fake. He didn't answer when they radioed him back. Then we got a call from a resident reporting two gunshots on the water."

"Who was the resident?"

Tim smiled ironically. "You know I can't divulge that."

"Yep. But I always have to try."

Matt thanked him and walked back to his car. He called Missy, who was finishing up her last appointment.

"Can you help me knock on some doors as soon as it's not too early to do it?" he asked.

"Why?"

Matt told her about the shooting and the boat that was allegedly dumping toxins.

"Pick me up at eight," she said.

CANVASSING from house to house was no one's favorite way of investigating. But Matt hoped they could speak with the person who called 911 about the gunshots. Maybe, just maybe, they had seen the boat in question or had other leads. He and Missy split up and rang doorbells of the homes along the Intracoastal Waterway near where the FWC officer's boat had been found after it had drifted into the mangroves.

He knew Missy would ask the right questions and take the right notes, even though she wasn't a reporter. The two of them had investigated enough strange occurrences for him to build trust in her.

Matt had tried five homes so far. Very nice homes, in fact, since they were worth millions of dollars. Two homes didn't answer his doorbell rings and knocks. One slammed the door in his face. The other two said they heard nothing last night.

Then he got a text from Missy.

Call me.

So he did.

"I found a home where the wife's mother heard gunshots around three in the morning while she was awake with insomnia," Missy said. "She stepped out on the patio and saw two boats touching each other. One had an insignia on the sides she couldn't read. It had a spotlight shining on the other boat, a large racing boat, she said. In her words, 'the kind of boat drug dealers with gold chains around their necks own.'"

Missy continued, "She saw one of the drug dealers: a really tall white guy with blond hair like a woman's, she said. I tried to get her to tell me more, but she said she was scared and went back inside right away."

"Did she report this to the police?" Matt asked.

"Yeah. They came by right before I did. I think she believed I was a cop, too. You know what doesn't make sense? Why would someone murder a law enforcement officer over this? Illegal dumping wouldn't have gotten these guys into that much trouble, especially since they were probably working for someone else."

"Some guys are just trigger-happy. And I would be willing to bet the shooter is on parole. Any arrest could send him back to prison."

"Someone would kill to avoid that?" By the tone of her voice, she knew the answer.

"Yes."

After about an hour more of canvassing yielded no more information, all they were left with were two facts: A large, high-powered boat was involved, and a tall, blond-haired man was aboard.

It was frustrating. That wasn't enough information to help at all. They needed more leads. And sadly, in Matt's experience, more leads often wouldn't come until more crimes had been committed.

Matt notified his editor at *The Jellyfish Beach Journal* and got the go-ahead to write the story about the murder. He called the detective leading the investigation for quotes and volunteered what they had learned about the blond-haired man. The detective already knew about him and told Matt to leave out those details, stating only that the police were seeking a person of interest.

Matt's story was the banner headline the next day and was picked up by wire services across Florida and even a few out-of-state newspapers.

The rise in manatee deaths was merely a little-noticed footnote.

3
TOXIC

The man was sunburned with thinning red hair and wire-rimmed spectacles. He faced Missy and Matt from behind a desk surrounded by stacks of clear-plastic boxes packed with jars of water samples and vegetation. He was Paul Velhorn, a regional director of the Florida Department of Environmental Protection.

"It's like playing whack-a-mole," he said. "We find a violation, track down the source, issue a fine, and the company doesn't pay. Then they or their trade association lobbies the government and the regulations are weakened. It's a miracle that the waters of Florida haven't become one giant, contaminated cesspool."

Matt, with his newspaper contacts, had secured the interview with Velhorn. Missy explained what had happened to the manatees.

"We think they were poisoned," Missy said, "but the blood work and tissue samples haven't shown a specific toxin. Do you think this resulted from pollutants?"

"It's true that manatee deaths have increased," Velhorn said, "and we can blame pollutants indirectly. Fertilizer runoff kills the sea grass that the manatees eat, and it also causes algae blooms, including red tide. The red tide is a major cause of manatee mortality."

"This manatee had no trace of red tide poisoning," Matt said. "Is there a particular chemical that kills them? Like boat fuel?"

Velhorn rested his chin on the steeple of his interlocked fingers. "Rarely. There were some studies that showed large concentrations of copper in deceased manatees. We instituted a regulation that reduced the amount of copper in herbicides and that helped the problem somewhat."

Missy was growing frustrated.

"So you admit there's a growing number of manatee deaths?"

"Yes," Velhorn said. "We attribute it to boat collisions and red tide."

"Okay, unrelated to manatees, can you give us a list of the worst polluters of the water in Florida?"

"Sure, I have a very familiar list," Velhorn said. He clicked away on his keyboard and three sheets of paper slid out of a laser printer. "You'll notice the list includes some air polluters, because particulates, such as mercury, end up in the water."

Missy and Matt thanked Velhorn and left the building.

"That wasn't very helpful. And there's almost a hundred names on this list," Missy said. "We can't possibly investigate all these sources."

"And I don't know how we'd investigate them. If we spoke to them, they'd deny everything."

"Well, let's start small," Missy said. "Let me figure out which company is located closest to where Seymour and Lubblubb were living. We'll figure out what to do from there."

Land along the Intracoastal Waterway is super-desirable. You'll find mansions, luxury condominiums, and a few parks. You won't find industrial polluters. Marinas along the waterway were responsible for some oil and gasoline leakage, but not on a grand scale.

The name on the list closest geographically to where Seymour and Lubblubb spent most of their time was the municipal wastewater treatment plant. It was at least three miles from the coast. But, studying a map, Missy noted it was located on the bank of a canal, part of a system meant to prevent inland flooding. In case of very heavy rains, the canals discharged water through sluice gates into the Intracoastal.

"It's got to be the treatment plant," Missy said in her kitchen.

"Yuck. You mean poo-poo and pee-pee are toxic to manatees?" Matt asked.

"There wasn't any of that in the water where we lived except for our own. And, well, from the fish," Seymour said. "And, heck, we manatees are vegetarians. How bad can our poo-poo be?"

"Bad. I had a vegetarian roommate after college," Matt said.

"The plant has been sanctioned for violating the Clean Waters Act," Missy said. "And yeah, I assume it's stuff from their plant leaking into the canal somehow. But maybe something worse than sewage is leaking as well?"

"What could be worse than sewage?" Matt asked.

"Something that kills manatees. I don't know, maybe some byproduct. Look, it's established that they're polluting regularly. They're bad actors."

"Or bad at repairing leaks in their pipes," Matt said.

"So what are you suggesting we do, Missy?" Seymour asked.

Missy realized she hadn't thought it through this far.

"Um, we surveil the place. Maybe we'll catch them dumping some chemicals. We could take samples of the water in the canal and have it tested."

"Sounds like a lot of work," Seymour said. When the other two gave him a judgmental look, he added, "Hey, y'all should know that manatees aren't lazy. Just because we're fat and float around all day." They continued staring at him. "Don't stereotype me."

"Who's up for joining me tonight on a mission?" Missy asked.

The two males glanced at each other and raised reluctant hands.

IT TURNED out to be easy to stake out a sewage treatment plant. When you thought about it, this was a place people would be least likely to want to break into. Missy figured even terrorists wouldn't want to bother blowing it up. If the proverbial poop hit the fan, it would end up raining on the terrorists. And what would be the strategic benefit?

The plant was on a main north-south road that crossed the canal. Right after the bridge was a grassy area next to the canal bank where Missy found easy parking. They sat in the dark on the bank across the canal from the plant and observed the well-lit property. There were clusters of giant, round tanks of varying heights connected by pipes. Several buildings were placed around the property. None of the three knew what they were for.

The wind shifted, bringing a ripe odor from the plant.

"Ah, the scent of raw sewage," Matt said.

"It's not as bad as raw," Missy said. "It's been partly treated. Let's say lightly simmered sewage."

"I'll never be able to get that image out of my brain," Matt said.

The three sat silently for several minutes until Missy realized it was just her and Matt.

"Where did Seymour go?" she asked.

"I didn't even realize he'd left. There's no moon, but with all the light across the way, we should have noticed him getting up and leaving."

"I hope he didn't go swimming."

"Yeah, not in this water. Should we go look for him?" Missy asked.

"No, he's a grownup. He knows what he's doing."

Matt sounded a little too happy that Seymour wasn't with them.

"He's really a grownup manatee," Missy said. "Our world is alien to him."

"He doesn't seem to have a hard time adjusting to it. And I'm surprised he speaks so proficiently. If he's been a manatee since he was a little kid, why hasn't his ability to speak atrophied over the years?"

"Why don't you ask him?"

"I will."

"Then go ahead and ask," Seymour said.

Missy jumped. Seymour was standing behind them.

"Where did you go?" she asked.

"I reconnoitered the grounds of the treatment plant," Seymour said. "There's hardly any security to speak of. I covered nearly the entire property. I saw nothing suspicious. But if they're dumping anything illegally, we'd have to spend multiple nights here in order to catch them."

"How did you sneak away from us and go all over the plant without being detected?" Matt asked.

"I have a little experience in reconnaissance and evasion."

"What?" Missy and Matt asked at the same time.

Seymour sat down on the canal bank beside Missy.

"I haven't been entirely honest with y'all," he said.

"Aren't you a mer-manatee?" Matt asked.

"I'm a shifter, yes. But I haven't been in full-time manatee form since I was young like I had told you. I shifted back and forth a heck of a lot since then. The truth is, I grew up as a human. Went to school. Joined the military. It was when I got back from Afghanistan that I decided to stay manatee permanently. By then, I'd had enough of the human species."

"Oh, great. A mysterious, brooding man with secrets," Matt muttered.

"And being in human form lately hasn't improved my opinion of humans," Seymour added.

"Okay, then," Missy said, getting to her feet. "I have plastic containers in the car. Let's gather some water samples and get out of here. If there's anything interesting in the results, we can stake out the plant nightly."

"Can't wait," Matt said sarcastically.

THE LAB that tested the water was expensive, especially with the rush charge added on. And it was all for naught. The test came back negative for any toxic substance. There was plenty of nitrogen and phosphorus from fertilizer runoff, and a trace of partly treated poo-poo and pee-pee. But nothing that raised any red flags.

Missy was clueless what they should do next. Until Matt called her the next day.

"I read on a wire service that there was a die-off of manatees," he said. "In the Santa Fe River, which is fed by natural springs. That's hundreds of miles from here."

"I have an idea," Missy said. "I know of certain individuals who are guardians of the springs. I'm going to try to speak with one and see if he knows of anyone poisoning the water."

"Who?"

"A gnome."

"Are you serious?"

"Absolutely. If anyone would know, it would be a gnome."

"Oh, boy. When do we leave?"

"I need to go on my own. Gnomes will only talk to humans who have some paranormal or supernatural abilities."

Missy had to leave right away to catch the moon in a quarter phase, the only time she could summon gnomes. She made the five-hour drive northwest to the Gainesville area to Ginnie Springs. She didn't know any gnomes up there, but did know there were several in the area. Gnomes from the Old Country guard gems, gold, silver, and other precious underground natural resources. In Florida, they were stewards of the pure, freshwater that bubbled up from underground. The spring water was of such high quality that corporations pumped it out in large quantities for bottling. Which angered the gnomes, but they haven't been able to stop it.

Missy hoped she could coax a gnome to reveal himself to her and help her with answers.

The park allowing access to the spring was closed at sunset, but she parked nearby, which was sufficient. As the quarter moon rose, she took out her bag of materials and searched the woods until she found a flat rock with an eastern exposure.

From her tote bag she took a pound of salt, several sprigs of rosemary, silver and gold coins, and a small cake. She poured a cup of ale and placed it on the rock. The last ingredient, as spelled out in the lore, was a can of Cheez Spray. She squirted a bit on her finger to make sure it worked. Finally, as the instructions ordered, she closed her eyes and cleared her mind of all thoughts impure. At her age, she didn't have many impure thoughts, but when she did, they involved chocolate.

Now there was nothing to do but wait in silence, kneeling on the dirt near the flat rock. Crickets chirped in the forest. Unseen small creatures rustled leaves. Mosquitoes whined in her ears. She wondered where she was going to sleep tonight as her exhaustion overtook her, and her chin kept dropping to her chest.

She snapped awake to the sounds of chewing. Then the gurgling of the Cheez Spray can, followed by the gulping of ale. All she could see in the darkness was the silhouette of a small, man-like creature squatting beside the rock. A loud belch signaled the summoning was successful.

"Oh, wise and honorable gnome, I seek your counsel."

"I figured," said a deep, scratchy male voice. He sounded like a large man, not a diminutive gnome. "What do you want?"

"As the guardian of these underground springs, can you tell me if there has been poisonings of your waters? I ask because I hear that manatees have died nearby."

A burst of curses came from the darkness, the likes of which she had never heard before. They would make even the crudest sailor cringe.

"Poison? It's not poison. It's black magic."

"Who cast this black magic?"

"I don't know who, and I don't know how. But I sensed it corrupting this pure water, and I was too late to stop it. Only humans would do something this vile. In time, it will fade from these waters, but it must not happen again."

"Do you have any clues to help me find who did it?"

"No, I don't."

"Do you have any advice?"

"Yes. Don't bring me Cheez Spray again that's past the expiration date."

4

BLACK MAGIC WOMAN

An email from the supernatural-friendly testing lab
was waiting in her inbox. It was divided into two
parts. The first had the results of Seymour's complete
blood count. It checked all the areas of the typical human blood
test, from red and white blood cell counts, hemoglobin, glucose,
cholesterol, liver enzymes, etc. By all measurements, Seymour
was in good health.

The second part of the report measured the levels of various
toxins in his blood. As the vet had said was the case with
Lubblubb's blood, there were no toxins at a dangerous level.
Just living in the modern world with all the human pollutants,
our bodies have traces of stuff you wouldn't want to know
about, from lead to nitrogen dioxide. Seymour did, too.

Besides the common toxins, the lab tested for materials that
were harmful for supernaturals, such as silver for werewolves
and garlic for vampires. It also flagged any unusual chemical or
compound found at a high level.

What grabbed Missy's eye was the staggeringly high level of

myristicin. The report had a footnote stating that while myristicin was an ingredient in insecticides and some hallucinogenic drugs, the presence of sabinene and camphene also in the blood sample point to one conclusion: nutmeg.

Seymour had been exposed to a high level of nutmeg?

Now, as far as she knew, nutmeg was harmless. What was it doing in the water of a marine estuary? Since the gnome had blamed black magic for polluting the water, she had to question whether the nutmeg was part of a potion. She had never used it with her own magick. But that didn't mean there weren't potions that did.

She did an internet search for spells and potions using nutmeg. After spending an hour, she found nothing interesting other than instructions for making a love potion and a bogus cure for colon cancer. The internet was useless for finding real spells and potions that actually worked. Witches and wizards don't like to share their proprietary secrets for free. They commit them to memory or keep them in grimoires. So be forewarned, that weight-loss spell you found through Google probably won't work.

Missy's practice of her magick was a solitary pursuit, and the only mentor she had to teach her was a wizard who was on the nutty side. This wizard had another shortcoming: He was dead. Dead, in fact, for nearly 400 years.

She began the frustrating experience of trying to summon the ghost of Don Mateo of Grenada. She had come into possession of a grimoire he had owned and added to, so his spirit was bound to her. He basically shared her home with her in his spectral way. But he usually showed up only when he wanted to.

"Don Mateo," she said aloud. "Don Mateo, can you please appear?"

There was no answer. Seymour let out a sob in the guest bathroom.

"Don Mateo, please appear. Or I will have to force you."

She waited for a while, sitting on her bed with her laptop. Nothing happened.

"Okay, you leave me no choice. I'm going to get the Red Dragon."

The Red Dragon was a small metal figurine shaped somewhat like a dragon. It was a magical talisman that amped up the power of her spells and had the power to make certain entities obey her. Like ghosts.

She got off the bed and went to retrieve the talisman which she kept hidden in a pouch at the bottom of a cat litter box, a place no thief would want to search.

As she walked across the floor toward the laundry room where the litter box was, she felt resistance in the air. And then something popped.

"At your service, my lady," said Don Mateo from behind her. He smiled devilishly amid his pointed beard as he stood in her bedroom beside her dresser. He had opened her underwear drawer.

"Leave my underwear alone," Missy said. "I need your expertise."

He bowed formally.

"Are you familiar with nutmeg?" she asked.

"The spice? Only slightly. It was quite expensive in Spain when I was alive. I also encountered some in America when I lived in San Marcos."

"Did you use it to make any potions?"

"No, not I. But I did hear of a witch in Havana who was famed for her deadly potions. It was rumored she used nutmeg to kill enemies and get rid of cold sores. She allegedly also used it in cake recipes. But I don't know if that was true."

"That's all you know?"

"Alas, yes."

"Okay, thanks for your help."

His apparition faded quickly and disappeared. But a pair of red panties rose from her drawer and floated out of her bedroom door.

Missy sighed. Her underwear would probably turn up someplace embarrassing, like on her front lawn, but nothing would rid the ancient ghost of his lingerie obsession.

The mention of Havana gave her an idea. The other source of magick advice she had was Luisa, the owner of a local *botanica* where Missy occasionally worked part time for extra cash. Luisa was a *bruja* as well as a Santeria priestess. She knew more about Caribbean and Latin American supernatural stuff than anyone.

"Seymour," she called out. "I have to run an errand. I'll be back shortly."

He answered with a sob that ended with the bubbling of bathwater.

The Jellyfish Beach Mystical Mart and *Botanica* was in an iffy part of town next to a check-cashing store and a storefront church. Bells tinkled when she opened the door and she was met with a cloud of incense.

"Ah, Missy, good to see you," Luisa said from behind the counter where the forty-ish Afro-Cuban cleaned a statuette of a Voodoo deity. "I didn't know you were working today."

"I'm here seeking your wisdom."

"Uh-oh, you're buttering me up. Now I'm frightened."

Missy laughed. "I was wondering if you know anything about nutmeg."

"It's just a spice. Sometimes I add it to my coffee."

"What about as an ingredient in a potion? You see, we found two manatees who were ill and beached themselves. One of them died. The other, who's a shifter, had large amounts of nutmeg in his system. So, I wondered if it had been used in a potion that sickened them."

Luisa's eyes grew wider and she uttered something foul in Spanish.

"You stay away from any potion like that," she said. "It is evil."

"What do you mean?"

"That's the kind of evil stuff obeah men use to curse their enemies."

Obeah was the black magic of the Caribbean. Technically, it was illegal, but it was practiced on all the islands, especially in the small villages of rural areas.

"Then I suppose I should call Carriacou Jack if I want more information," Missy said.

"He's the only obeah man I know," Luisa said. She tried to smile, but apprehension still narrowed her eyes.

Carriacou Jack, whose actual name was Jack Wilson, was a real estate agent who moonlighted as an obeah man for clients in the Miami area. Missy met him a couple of years ago when he was hired to hunt down a soucouyant, the female vampire of the French West Indies.

Missy thanked Luisa, and when it was obvious that the *botanica* owner didn't want to get involved in this matter, Missy decided to call Carriacou Jack from her car.

"Trident Realty, Jim Wilson here," he answered in a rich Caribbean accent.

"Hi Mr. Wilson, this is Missy Mindle from Jellyfish Beach. Do you remember me?"

"Ah, the witch. Yes, I remember you. It was that matter with the soucouyant. You got trapped in your own snare spell, didn't you?" He chuckled.

"Something like that. Do you have a moment? I have a question for you."

"My pleasure."

She repeated the story about the sickened manatees and the traces of nutmeg in the tissue.

"Nutmeg won't kill an animal," she said. "But it might if it was in a magic potion. Do you know of any like that?"

The sharp intake of his breath hissed on her ear. "That's bad news, that kind of spell. I know an obeah man who killed his enemy's goats that way."

"Would it work by dumping it in a large body of water?"

"I can't say for sure, but I don't see why not. It can make a powerful potion, from what I've heard, if created with the right magic."

"Do know of any obeah men here in Florida who could do it?"

"Not personally, but there are probably some. But killing animals or people like that is not easy to get away with in this country. And, you know, it doesn't have to be an obeah man who did this. You just have to know your black magic really well."

"Is there an antidote for this potion, a way to neutralize it?"

"No. Not with that kind of magic. The only way to stop it is to stop the sorcerer who's making it."

"But how do I find this sorcerer?"

"Use your magic."

Unfortunately, Missy didn't know where to begin.

MATT CALLED the next morning after Missy returned home from patient visits. He tried to make it seem casual, as if he were just saying hi, but it was obvious he wanted to know if Seymour was misbehaving.

"He's still in deep mourning," Missy said. She went on to tell Matt about what the gnome had revealed, the discovery of the nutmeg, and what the obeah man had told her.

"You mean someone literally dumped a magic potion in the Intracoastal to kill Seymour's mate?"

"Not to kill her specifically, but to kill manatees. Maybe other wildlife as well, but I've done some research and haven't found any mentions of fish or bird kills in the area. What I did find was that manatee deaths have increased overall in the state. The number killed by boats is up, but also unexplained mortalities."

"I get the feeling you're on the road to a conspiracy theory."

"I don't have a theory. I just want to know why someone dumped a black-magic potion in the Intracoastal Waterway and elsewhere."

"Well, to make you feel better, I'll search news archives and see if anything stands out."

"It's not to make me feel better. It's to keep more manatees from dying."

Afterwards, she thought about her conversation with Carriacou Jack. He had recommended she use her magick. How could her magic help?

Sometimes with magick, you just had to go with it and see where it led you. Magick wasn't a rigid set of rules; it was a process of discovery. It even taught you some things about yourself along the way.

Missy had an idea, but she didn't know if it would work.

She looked for Seymour in the guest bathroom, but he

wasn't there. She knocked on his bedroom door and a low mumble came forth. She opened the door a crack. Seymour lay in bed beneath the covers.

"I'm happy to see you're giving the bed a try," she said.

"The tub wasn't comfortable. It's too small, and the surface is hard. It's not like floating weightlessly in the water."

"As a human, you'll be learning a lot of truths like that. You're not a manatee anymore."

"I want to be one again. As soon as I can shift back, I'm out of here." He sat up in the bed, concern on his face. "Not that you haven't been a wonderful hostess. I do appreciate all your help. I wish there was a way to repay you."

"No need. All I want is to find out what made you and Lubblubb sick. And why you haven't been able to shift. Have you tried recently?"

"Yes. While you were out, I went to the canal across the street."

"And trespassed on my neighbor's property again."

"Animals don't recognize human property deeds. Anyway, I've been feeling much better lately. Stronger and more like myself. So I swam in the canal and tried to shift, and it wouldn't happen. It's so frustrating, like I lost the ability. I kept trying until an alligator took notice and swam toward me. They rarely bother manatees, but this guy had me in his sights. Another disadvantage of being human."

"I suspect there's black magic involved," Missy said. "Your blood work showed large amounts of nutmeg, which shouldn't be there. You obviously ingested it somewhere, and I think it was dumped into the water deliberately. Since it's an ingredient in certain black-magic potions, I'm looking into that theory."

"A magic potion? Why?"

"Possibly to kill manatees."

"But why?"

"That's what we need to find out. Let me see your arm. I want to take another blood sample. Just a small one this time."

She pulled a chair up next to the bed and withdrew one vial of blood. She taped a cotton ball over the spot.

"I'm going to perform my magick in the kitchen now. And I don't mean making a fantastic meal. So please stay away. I need privacy."

Seymour nodded, and Missy brought the vial to the kitchen where she drew a large circle on the white tile with a black dry-erase marker. She knelt within it and placed five tea candles around the circumference of the circle, a candle at each point of an imagined pentagram, and lit them.

She touched her forehead to the floor while she held the Red Dragon talisman in her left hand and the vial of blood in her right. Then she put herself into a trance-like state and gathered the energies from within her, as well as from the five elements of earth, fire, water, air, and spirit. The energies coalesced into a mighty ball of power in her solar plexus.

It was time to begin the spell.

She quietly uttered the words in Hebrew of a questing spell she had learned. Call it diagnostic witchcraft. It sensed the presence of any kind of magic, whether it be a spell cast upon her or on an object. Or in a vial of blood.

The vial grew warmer in her right hand. There was definitely a trace of magic in Seymour's blood. But what kind and for what?

She needed to increase the efficacy of the spell. And that's where the Red Dragon came in. It was like an external battery pack of magical energy.

She whispered the final words of the spell and a strong

tingling, uncomfortable like a mild electrical shock, began in her left hand and ran up her arm until it reached her heart.

Her heartbeat quickened, and a surge of vigor and euphoria spread through her body. It reached her head, and her scalp broke out in goosebumps. Her hair stood on end. She was on fire with unbelievable power.

Most important, the clarity of her mind increased. She absorbed every detail of the kitchen, even with her eyes closed: every speck of dust, every crack or chip, the way the morning sun left a warm glow upon the counter. She smelled weeks of cooking odors. She sensed the life of every dust mite and bacterium. Her perception felt superhuman.

And then she turned this perception upon the blood vial in her hand. Upon the power that infected the blood.

She saw the truth immediately. Yes, it was black magic. It was meant to mimic the toxic effects of pesticides: the impairment of breathing and damage to the nervous system. It was a strong spell that wouldn't fade in time, but would be eventually dispersed in the water where the potion had been poured and would be excreted from the body via urine over time. But death usually happened before the body could eliminate it.

Moreover, it was evil magic. It took its power not from the natural energies of the earth, but from the power of death, disease, decay, and destruction. From the hatred in human hearts. From greed, gluttony, and the other deadly sins. It was empowered with the aid of a demon of some sort that had most likely been conjured by the sorcerer.

The vial of blood was so hot the skin of her palm was burning. She almost dropped it, but not yet. She had to search deeper.

What was the purpose of the potion?

To kill.

To kill what?

Manatees.

Why kill manatees?

Because it has been commanded.

Who commanded it?

Missy could get no answer, but that wasn't surprising. No sorcerer of any skill would allow information like that to get into a spell.

Why is it necessary to kill manatees?

Missy cringed as the answer swept over her, darkening her soul and filling her with despair. For there was no answer other than because evil is evil. Death begets death. And all the Seven Deadly Sins wreak their havoc upon the earth, unless they're stopped.

Wow, Missy thought, this is depressing. Why would anyone want to practice black magic?

She placed the blood vial and the talisman on the floor, then wiped away a section of the circle she had drawn to break the spell. Her right hand still throbbed from the burning sensation, but her palm looked undamaged. Her knees were aching from kneeling on the tile, so she swung her legs around and sat cross-legged.

Middle-aged knees were not meant to be kneeling on the floor. She should use a cushion or a yoga mat. Somehow that seemed kind of lame for spell casting, but what choice did she have? Painful knees mess up her game.

So how was she going to find out who had created the black-magic potion, since she couldn't find out forensically?

She only knew one person who practiced black magic, so naturally this possibility was floating in her brain. But she tried to suppress it, hoping it couldn't be. There had to be plenty of black-magic practitioners in Florida, right? Every other ne'erdo-well ends up in this state. Why not evil sorcerers? She hoped the culprit was anyone other than the person she had in mind.

Because that person was her mother.

No, not the mother who raised her. Missy had been adopted as an infant and had a perfectly normal, if boring, childhood. But she recently discovered the true identity of her birth parents. Her father had been a powerful witch who adhered to benevolent white magick. He died in suspicious circumstances shortly after Missy was born. Her mother, whom she thought had also died, turned out to be alive. Also a witch, she had turned to the dark side.

Her mother, who went by the alias of Ruth Bent, lived in rural Central Florida and sold her evil magic to the highest bidder. She would do anything for a buck, and Missy once had to convince her to dispel a demon she had summoned. The "convincing" turned into her mother trying to kill her with black magic and Missy barely survived.

But aren't all mother-daughter relationships like that?

To make matters worse, Missy had recently heard from a cousin (whom she also didn't know she had) that her mother may have played a role in her father's mysterious death, and the role may have involved summoning a demon.

Please, please, please don't let this potion be my mother's handiwork, Missy begged an Almighty Power who didn't seem to be listening.

I can't deal with my mother right now. Please allow me to pretend she doesn't exist.

She drew some comfort in the fact that it would be too much of a coincidence that her mother was involved with this case.

Right?

5

VAMPIRE REPELLENT

Missy drove across the drawbridge over the Intracoastal Waterway and soon turned into the mainland residential areas. Her headlights pierced the darkness along streets where everyone was asleep. Even early joggers and dog walkers weren't up yet.

She was exhausted. Her overnight shift had included eleven patient visits, each one more frustrating than the previous. Cantankerous vampire seniors are not easy to work with. Taking blood samples from reluctant human patients is never easy, but when they're vampires, you have the difficulty of finding a decent vein. Vampire blood itself is very viscous and hard to draw, often clogging the needle. And then, you have the delicate dance of avoiding the vampire's instinctual hunger at the sight and smell of blood, even if it's their own.

Tonight, a seventy-eight-year-old widow from Pittsburgh named Sharon nearly chomped onto Missy's throat. Missy had sensed the arousal coming, had seen Sharon's pupils dilate and her nostrils flare after seeing her blood ooze slowly into the vial. But there wasn't enough collected yet. Just a centimeter more and she'd be finished. Missy was about to pull the needle and wipe the insertion site with alcohol when a sudden movement made her rear back. Sharon caught herself as she was striking and pulled back. But those fully extended fangs came way too close to Missy's jugular veins for comfort.

Missy had always felt she deserved hazard pay. She made a bit more than a home health nurse for humans, but not enough to compensate for the risks she took.

The amulet she wore around her neck that was supposed to ward off vampire attacks was of her own construction based on her own knowledge of witchcraft. Acceptance Home Care hadn't provided it or reimbursed her for the cost of the rare herbs, oils, and powders used to create the magick potpourri inside the cloth sack.

If Missy hadn't been a witch, the only thing protecting her would have been the company's vague promise that the vampires at Squid Tower had strict rules not to feed on their nurses. Like that was sufficient. No wonder it was a high-turnover job. Missy had never learned what happened to the nurses who had served before her and why they left. Her patients would never say, either. After a while, Missy realized it was best she didn't know.

So she drove home at 3:30 a.m., hoping to get some sleep before she had to return to the beach to see werewolf patients at Seaweed Manor next door to Squid Tower. Her first appointment was at 10:00 a.m., which meant not enough sleep. The werewolves there were not fully nocturnal like the vampires, but when they shifted to wolves, they stayed up through the night. When they didn't shift, many stayed up late to party, making them avoid early morning appointments with Missy. She preferred to schedule her last vampire appointment just before dawn and her first werewolf patient just after dawn. That made her life much easier.

She was almost nodding off at the wheel. Finally, she came to her street and rolled slowly along, her headlights reflected in the eyes of a feral cat before it disappeared behind a hedge. She pulled into her driveway and turned off the engine.

Something was wrong. She was not alone.

She sat for a while, doors locked, head swiveling to search for anyone out there. The light on her front porch only made things worse, creating scary shadows from the palm fronds swaying in the slight breeze.

She couldn't sit in the car forever. She turned off the switch of the overhead light above her so it wouldn't turn on when she opened the car door. With her hand firmly on the can of pepper spray she carried in her purse, she quickly opened the door and jumped out.

A cat yowled two houses down. A large, dark shape moved across the street in pursuit of the cat.

Missy's chest clenched in fear. No, it couldn't be. Didn't the large shape resemble a bear? Yes, an enormous bear. Rather like the vampire cave bear the Neanderthal vampires had kept as a pet but allowed to escape and terrorize neighborhoods.

This was not good. She had to get inside.

But a woman blocked her path. A vampire. She bared her fangs and hissed, circling Missy, trying to lunge at her but held back by the magick of Missy's amulet.

Missy recognized the young woman. She was one of the recovering drug addicts the Neanderthals kept enslaved to feed upon. But they had turned this one into a vampire.

"Stay away," Missy said. As if that was going to do any good.

"You killed my maker," the young woman said. "You will die now for that."

The vampire kept circling, moaning in her hunger, looking more and more bestial as her cravings and frustration contorted her face. She growled.

Missy tried to move toward her front door, but the vampire pressed ever closer to her. Missy feared the power of the amulet would not be enough to protect her. The vampire's hunger was going to overcome the magick.

She must not know how to mesmerize me, Missy thought. She's just going to attack me like an animal.

Missy shot a stream of pepper spray into the eyes of the vampire. The creature howled in pain, but the chemical was not affecting her like it would a human.

Missy dropped her tote bag, reached into her left pocket, and grasped the power charm she always carried to enhance her magick. It wasn't as strong as the Red Dragon talisman, which she rarely carried as it was too rare to risk losing.

She quickly recited the words of a protection spell to create a shield around her. That was her only chance to fend off the attacks until she could come up with a better tactic. The energy began to take shape and solidify around her.

But the vampire struck like a rattlesnake before the spell was complete. She knocked Missy to the ground, clawing at her, growling, pushing her snapping jaws toward Missy's neck. The cord of the amulet broke and slipped away.

Missy struggled to keep the fangs from her flesh. But even though the vampire was weakened from hunger, she was stronger than a human.

Somehow, Missy wriggled out from beneath the vampire and crawled toward the front door. And then, sharp pain flared in her right calf.

She's been cut by the vampire's nails, breaking her skin. Releasing blood that would only inflame the monster more.

The vampire went for her leg in a frenzy. Missy kicked her in the jaw, snapping her head backwards. But it only caused a brief pause.

The growling creature leaped and landed full-length upon Missy's back, partially knocking the wind out of her. She yanked Missy by the hair, exposing her neck. She felt defenseless lying on her stomach.

Missy groped along the ground with both hands, searching for a rock, anything, to use as a weapon.

Her right hand found a small, smooth metal object. It was the post to her home-security yard sign. She remembered it had a sharpened end to make it easy to drive into the ground.

It was, in effect, a stake.

She yanked it from the ground and twisted her body so she could drive it into the vampire's chest.

The vampire swatted her hand and sent the sign flying into the yard. Then she sank her fangs into Missy's forearm.

The pain was raw and burning as the vampire slurped the blood, rubbing her body against Missy's almost sexually.

Do not panic, Missy told herself. Think of magick. Think of the power within you. Think of the earth and the energy you can draw upon. Think of the paranormal gifts God has given you.

Her telekinesis. Mind over matter. Normally, she used it for moving objects mentally, sometimes amplified by a spell. Maybe it could buy her a little time.

She focused as much as she could, gathering energies. She uttered a simple invocation, a catalyst for the magical reaction.

And with her mind, she flung the vampire off her. It slammed against the car and rolled over the hood. Stopping the vampire from drinking blood would prevent her from getting stronger. But it was only a temporary fix.

Missy reached into her pocket for the power charm. She recited the Latin words of her sleeping spell. She'd never used it against a vampire before, but it had worked with an ogre in the past.

It didn't work.

The vampire came running around the car at her.

Missy used her telekinesis to trip the creature and roll it away from her. She couldn't save her life with the telekinesis alone, and it required all her concentration, preventing her from casting a new spell.

Headlights approached along the street. It was probably the newspaper delivery person. She prayed for it to move faster.

The driver flung the newspaper, wrapped in its plastic bag, at her driveway. It hit the vampire.

Then Missy flung the vampire into the street.

With a sickening crunch, the car ran over her.

The car stopped, and the driver got out.

"She jumped in front of me! I swear that's what happened. My life is over now."

He bent to look at the body beneath his car, sobbing loudly.

Until he was knocked in the air and landed on Missy's lawn

The vampire, unscathed, sprinted up the driveway toward Missy.

By now, her protection spell had kicked in. This time, it was complete when the vampire lunged at her.

She bounced off the invisible bubble like she had slammed into Plexiglass.

Missy began building a binding spell which, if it worked, would hold the vampire immobile until dawn arrived and the rising sun destroyed the creature.

But she had second thoughts. This young woman had been trying to stay sober when she was betrayed and handed over to be food for vampires. She was turned against her will and now her maker was dead, thanks to Missy. She was alone in the world with no guidance or comfort.

Maybe if she kept the vampire at bay, she would leave on her own before dawn.

Missy slowly retreated backwards toward her front porch while the vampire made repeated lunges, crashing into the protection bubble. Missy drew upon more power and strengthened the spell. She could maintain it indefinitely now.

After more attempts, the vampire finally saw the writing on the wall. And the reddish tinge in the eastern sky.

She finally turned away to find a safe hiding spot. But before she left, she took a bite of the unconscious paper boy and fed for a while. Then she fled.

Missy waited until sunrise arrived before she undid the protection spell. She was about to call an ambulance for the paper boy, but he stumbled to his feet. When he saw that whoever he had struck was nowhere in sight. He quickly drove away.

Maybe he thought it had all been a bad dream.

MARIA AWOKE at sunset in the garden shed behind the vacant home down the street from the witch. She curled up against the thick fur of Lucy, the cave bear. The small amount of human blood she'd consumed helped restore some of the strength she'd lost on her diet of blood from small animals and rodents. But she couldn't go on like this.

Getting revenge on the witch would have to wait for another night. She needed to dine on a human who wouldn't fight back.

Hunting in the suburbs was a waste of time. She said goodbye to Lucy and promised to return to her soon, then set out walking south on the residential roads. She didn't know the area well, having been a virtual shut-in during her drug recovery period, and after that, she was held as a prisoner by the vampires. But since she was not far from the beach, she was certain to get to a more urban area before long.

Once she was there, prey would be abundant and her risk of standing out was much slimmer.

As she approached Jellyfish Beach's small downtown, traffic increased. The headlights hurt her eyes. Soon, people appeared on the sidewalks. In the next block were neon signs of restaurants and bars. Groups of humans crossed the streets.

Her stomach rumbled. All that fresh blood ripe for the taking.

But she didn't know how to take down a victim in public, and she was too frightened to try. She turned into an alley and found dark shadows behind a dumpster. Maybe if she waited here, a human would come along.

Cigarette smoke drifted her way. She peered around the dumpster. A human stood at the alley's entrance. His back was toward her as he smoked. If she were quick, she could grab him and drag him back to the shadows for feeding.

But what if he screamed? She hadn't yet learned how to mesmerize prey. So all she knew how to do was use overwhelming force. How could she get away with that in public like this?

This was actually worse than in the suburbs. There, a woman walking alone at night drew too much attention, and there rarely was prey about that wasn't locked inside cars. But here in town, she suffered from sensory overload. The headlights and streetlights hurt her eyes. The motorcycles and laughing crowds were deafening. And the smells overwhelmed her: car exhaust, garlic, perfume, sweat, food rotting in the dumpster.

The man at the end of the alley swayed slightly as he stood there. He was drunk. Maybe he'd be easier to subdue than she thought. She moved cautiously toward him.

The cigarette smoke almost made her gag, but through it she caught the scent of his body and hair, healthy and clean aside from the alcohol. No trace of any cancer or disease like that.

She crept closer, hugging the left wall of the alley and its shadows. She was over forty feet away but could hear his heart-beat, his blood coursing through his arteries and veins. His sharp intakes of cigarette smoke. A gurgling in his stomach. The swallow of saliva.

The predator in her was going mad, causing her heart to race and her mind to forget everything other than this creature in front of her and the nurturing blood he held beneath a thin layer of skin.

He was like fast food that wasn't bad for you.

Her sneaker scuffed the crumbling asphalt. She froze, waiting to make sure he hadn't heard.

"I wouldn't do that if I were you."

The voice came from the shadows of parallel drainpipes running up the bricks behind a building.

The woman was a vampire! Maria could sense it instantly.

"Why?" Maria asked.

"Are you new around here?"

"Yes."

"Something tells me you're new at hunting, too."

"Yes," Maria confessed. "My maker was destroyed shortly after she turned me."

"Ah, a babe in the wood, are you? My name is Sylvia. And you are?"

"Maria."

"No offense, but you look like you've been sleeping outside. Are you homeless?"

"I have nothing. I'm alone except for my pet."

"Vampires don't have pets."

"My maker's clan did. A vampire cave bear."

"Ah, you were part of the clan of Neanderthals that was trying to take over the town. We were all worried about them, but it seems the only vampires they could rule were a bunch of geezers at the beach."

"Yes. I was their prisoner before they turned me. And then they were all destroyed."

"I'm sorry about your maker, but in Florida, we vampires don't take well to being ruled. They've got the Cuban vampire mafia trying to run things in Miami and the Vampire Guild up in San Marco. A similar guild in Tampa. Other than that, it's the Wild West in Florida. No rules, but it also means vampires like you can slip through the cracks and suffer needlessly. Do you need a place to stay?"

Maria nodded.

"Come along with me then. I live in a small hive in a house a few blocks from here. I'll make sure you feed tonight. If the others in the hive take well to you, you can stick around, and I'll show you the ropes."

"Thank you so much."

Sylvia's words were the sweetest she'd heard since Maria had gone into recovery.

She followed Sylvia along some backstreets to a north-south street lined with tall oaks and palm trees. A few blocks north of the main drag was a decrepit two-story stucco house.

"Welcome to our humble abode," Sylvia said.

The yard was overgrown and strewn with trash. When they went inside, the air was musty and laden with mildew.

"It appears my hive-mates aren't here right now. They must be out hunting."

"Is that what you were doing when you found me?" Maria asked.

"Yes. But when I say hunting, I don't mean stalking and attacking prey in the open. We prefer the spider's method: Let your prey blunder into your trap and then feed upon them in the privacy of your own home. It's the only safe way to do it nowadays. There are too many people and security cameras everywhere to feed in some alleyway."

"But I don't understand," Maria said. "What is your trap?"

Sylvia smiled, but didn't answer. She walked through the house, peering into each room. She stopped at a sunroom in the back of the first floor. Filled with windows to let in the natural light the vampires would never appreciate, it had plant shelves covered with empty pots, a love seat and a few chairs.

A young man sprawled across the love seat, his head canted backwards, drool running down his cheek.

"Look," Sylvia said. "A fly has blundered into our web."

Maria's gut clenched. The man was obviously stoned out of his mind, probably on opiates.

"You give them drugs?" Maria asked.

"Exactly. Please help yourself to dinner. But don't drain him. My hive-mates might have struck out tonight."

"I can't," Maria said.

"What do you mean? Have you not fed on a human yet?"

"It's not that. I was an addict for years. It almost killed me. I was in recovery, finally. I worked so hard to be clean. If he has drugs in his blood, I just can't."

"I've never had any effect from drugs in the systems of my prey."

"But I might. I'm more vulnerable than you. Or even if I don't, I don't want impure blood in me. I can't explain, but all my hopes and dreams are about being clean."

"A girl has to eat," Sylvia said. "There's a young, healthy stud right there, probably loaded with iron and platelets. He's what's on the menu of our establishment. You can enjoy, or go hungry. It's up to you."

Sylvia gave a fake smile and started to leave the room before adding, "In any event, please stay here, come morning. It's dangerous out there."

Maria nodded, and Sylvia left the room.

The man remained unmoving except for the rise and fall of his breathing.

Her stomach growled. When she was human, she had never imagined that vampires' stomachs did that.

6

BARBARIAN BOAT WORKS

I t was a thirty-five-foot workboat with an open stern deck and low gunnels, which made it easier to dump the fifty-gallon barrels into the Intracoastal Waterway. Pierre and Tom did the grunt work, while Carlos was at the helm keeping the boat pointing into the current.

"Dang, this stuff sure smells bad," Tom said. "Anybody know what it is?"

"Industrial waste. What else?" Pierre said. "The factory dumps it into the river all day long."

"Then why do we have to bring this stuff all the way out here?"

"Because it's really bad stuff."

"Won't it kill the fish?" Tom asked. "I want to bring my kid out here to fish when he's old enough."

"I've been doing this for months," Carlos said. "I haven't seen any reports of fish kills."

"Why are we always doing it in no-wake manatee speed zones?"

"That's just a coincidence," Carlos replied. "Most of the Intracoastal around here is a no-wake zone. I think it's because all these rich people in their waterfront mansions don't want their seawalls damaged."

"It's not to protect the manatees?" Tom asked.

"It's to take all the fun out of boating," Carlos said.

"Stop your chatting and help me with this next barrel," Pierre said.

It was back-breaking work, lifting the heavy plastic white barrel, resting its side against the gunnel, then carefully tipping over enough to let the foul-smelling liquid slosh into the water.

"It smells worse than farts," Tom said. "It smells like pumpkin-spice ale that went bad months ago."

Just then, they were blinded by a spotlight. They froze.

It was the Sheriff's marine patrol.

"What are you boys doing?" asked a folksy voice over a loudspeaker.

Tom shouted, "We're just dumping some chemicals, officer."

"You idiot," Carlos said in a low voice. "It's chum. We're dumping chum," he shouted to the man behind the blinding spotlight.

"Chum? There's no fish in here that you need fifty gallons of chum to catch. Well, I'll let you waste your chum. But tell me, you boys aren't smuggling dope, are you?"

"No, sir!" all three responded in unison.

"You aren't smuggling in any illegals, are you? Any Cubans or Haitians?"

"No sir," Carlos said. "No Cubans or Haitians on this boat."

"Hey, I'm Haitian," Pierre said, "and proud of it."

"A Haitian?" asked the voice on the loudspeaker.

"Thracian," Carlos said. "He's a Thracian from Thrace. It was an ancient country, now part of Greece, Turkey, and Bulgaria."

"I'm coming aboard," said the marine patrol officer.

LIKE MOST LOCAL NEWSPAPERS, The Jellyfish Beach Journal was no longer independently owned. A large media conglomerate, Three Star Media Group, had purchased it. The benefit to Matt as a reporter was that he could access all news content from the dozens of local papers owned by the conglomerate.

Each day, in between deadlines, he had looked for stories of dead manatees found throughout the state. Unfortunately, these stories appeared regularly, in locations along the Intracoastal Waterway that ran along the entire east coast of Florida, in the lagoons the waterway traversed, or the rivers that fed into it. Manatee deaths also occurred in the rivers that flowed from the freshwater natural springs in the center of the state, and in the estuaries along the Gulf coast. In short, wherever manatees lived in Florida, manatees were dying. It was depressing to see the extent of it.

Matt also searched for stories about companies fined or cited for illegal pollution. It turns out this didn't happen much in recent years, though Matt suspected this was because of lax enforcement rather than less polluting.

So it naturally caught his eye when he came across a story about a boat seized that was suspected of smuggling migrants. No one was charged. He almost missed it, but the article mentioned the boat had been dumping contents of fifty-gallon drums into the Intracoastal Waterway. The substance being dumped was never identified.

That sounded eerily similar to the incident when the FWC officer was murdered. Could they be dumping the magic potion that Missy had identified? It seemed crazy to think of a potion being produced in quantities large enough to fit in fifty-gallon drums. This wasn't some old crone making a pot of magic in a shack hidden in the woods. This was magic on an industrial scale. Matt could barely comprehend it.

The article said the boat was registered to Barbarian Boat Works. A quick internet search revealed that the company manufactured a popular line of pleasure and fishing boats, and their main factory was in Florida.

Odds were that the boat crew was dumping industrial waste. Illegal dumping was, unfortunately, a common way to cut costs. It happened all the time, everywhere. Matt doubted a boat manufacturer would be involved in making magic potions.

He called Missy and reported his findings.

"Of course, a boat company!" Missy said. "Why didn't I think of that?"

"Why *would* you think of that?"

"Boats are the biggest killer of manatees in Florida."

"So why would they want to kill more of them? It makes no sense. Why make a huge public relations problem worse? The more endangered manatees become, the greater the blame the boat industry gets."

"Yeah, I guess you're right," Missy said. "But we need to look into this, anyway."

"I can look into their record on illegal dumping and such. But how do we find out if they're manufacturing black-magic potions?"

"If I can get inside their factory, I can sense if there's any magic around."

"And how do we get you inside their factory?"

"Through lies and subterfuge. That's why we make a great team, Matt. We're good at bluffing our way into information."

"Dishonesty will get you everywhere. But this time, you're going to be the one who does it."

As a home health nurse, Missy was not exactly overflowing with cash. In fact, the vampire clients of Acceptance Home Care were notoriously cheap (the werewolves, trolls, and others weren't as bad). That meant Missy was not eager to spend money on investigating anything. But having committed to finding justice for Lubblubb, she forked out the payment for a van rental. It was a nondescript, unmarked white van, because she was pretending to be a contract delivery person for internet shipments.

The Barbarian Boat Works factory was west of Jellyfish beach in an industrial park. The factory was on a small river that winded its way to the Intracoastal, and it undoubtably carried spilled fuel, paint, and other chemicals from the plant that ended up in the river, intentionally or not.

Up ahead was a security gate. She hadn't counted on that. When the van pulled up to the guard booth, a middle-age woman with thick eyeglasses looked up from her tablet.

"UPSP," Missy said, holding up a fake package.

The guard didn't realize there was no such thing as UPSP and went back to the video on her tablet. The gate arm rose. Missy probably shouldn't have burned rubber as she raced to get past the gate.

Her plan was to get inside the factory, or at least as close to it as possible. It all depended upon where the delivery dock was. The entrance road went around a large parking lot, then cut toward the complex. There was a clear difference between the office building and the gigantic, boxy assembly plant. A sign that said "deliveries" pointed to an entrance between the two buildings. Instead, she took a right into the plant area. She almost collided with a forklift that carried a new boat, wrapped in plastic, to join others in a line beside the building.

She parked the van next to the boats and walked briskly through a giant garage-style door. The manufacturing floor spread out before her, with boats in different stages of assembly. No one noticed her, at least so far.

Still holding her dummy package, she closed her eyes and cleared her mind. She didn't need to cast a complicated spell. She didn't need to analyze blood for traces of black magic.

All she needed was to use her magick to engage her extrasensory ability to pick up the presence of magic, especially black magic. Normally, it wasn't hard to sense.

"Hey, lady! Can I help you? You can't be in here without a hardhat."

Footsteps approached.

She opened her eyes as a man with a hardhat and a shirt with the company logo bore down upon her.

She had sensed nothing. There was no magic here at all.

"Sorry," she said to the man. "I had a package to deliver."

"Next building," he said, pointing to her left.

"Okay. Thank you."

She walked out of the factory and drove the van through the gate.

Just because there wasn't any magic here didn't mean this company wasn't involved, she told herself. There had to be another location where the potion was made.

7

DOMESTIC BLISS

Missy's doorbell rang, knocking her out of a deep sleep. She glanced at the bedside clock. It was 7:00 a.m., just an hour after she had gone to sleep. She pulled on a T-shirt and sweatpants and stumbled to the front door.

It was Morty, her neighbor from across the street. He was short and thin with a stooped posture, probably in his late seventies, early eighties. Some people prefer neighbors who are observant, who will make sure no one breaks into your house when you're away. Morty was not that kind of neighbor. He spent all his time in front of the television watching political news shows. Aliens could land a spaceship in Missy's front yard, and Morty wouldn't notice.

In that way, Morty was the perfect neighbor for Missy, with all the crazy stuff that happened to her. From magic-induced sinkholes appearing in her yard to vampire attacks, it was all beyond Morty's attention or caring.

Except today.

"Good morning," he said. "Sorry to come by so early, but there's a naked man in the canal behind my house. It's your friend."

Seymour was up to his nonsense again.

"Oh, that's Seymour. My cousin."

"I saw him floating face-down," Morty said. "I thought he was dead. Then he came up for air."

"Seymour is so quirky, isn't he?"

"He's not quirky. He's a perv. Tell him to wear a bathing suit. What if my cleaning lady was here? She would quit if she saw that."

"I'm sorry. I'll tell him. Seymour is one of those naturalists."

"He's a weirdo. Tell him there's alligators in there. They could bite off something that's precious to him."

"I'll tell him."

"And next time he walks through my yard, I'll call the police."

"I'm sorry for disturbing you. I don't plan for my cousin to stay with me much longer."

As Morty crossed the street to return to his home and his news shows, he met Seymour headed the opposite way, dripping with water, strands of hydrilla tangled in his sparse hair.

They had words. Missy couldn't hear them. Morty shook his finger at him. Seymour spread his arms, palms out, in innocence. Morty wagged his finger more sternly. Then he pointed at Seymour's privates. Seymour looked down, as if just discovering they were there. A look of comprehension came over his face. He smiled, waved goodbye and continued around the side of Missy's house to her back porch.

She fetched a towel from the linen closet and tossed it to him, diverting her eyes.

"My neighbor Morty doesn't want you skinny-dipping in the canal anymore," she said.

"That man is too uptight."

"He has a point. You trespassed through his property and the police could arrest you for exposing yourself. Which you're doing right now. Will you wrap yourself with the towel, please?"

"Sorry," he said glumly.

"And there are alligators in there."

"I know how to avoid gators. And I didn't see any around."

"I'm sorry I don't have a swimming pool. The Jellyfish Beach Municipal Pool is only a twenty-minute walk away. You could go there. But you have to wear a bathing suit."

"I don't like chlorinated water."

"Then go swimming at the beach. You know, it's time we talked about how long you're going to stay here."

"I thought we already discussed this," Seymour said. "We need to find out who poisoned Lubblubb and make sure they're punished. Then, we need to fix whatever is keeping me from shifting back to a manatee."

"We may never find that." That wasn't entirely true; Missy didn't know any spells to make him shift, but that didn't mean it wasn't possible.

"Where am I supposed to go? I don't have a job. I don't have a bank account. I don't have a phone. I don't have identification. I don't even have a subscription to a streaming service. How am I supposed to survive out in the world?"

"You had a life before. You were in the military. Can't you restore your previous identity?"

"I don't know how. When I decided to become a manatee permanently, I gave away all my stuff. Sold my parents' home. Donated all my money to charity. Then I burned my credit cards and driver's license. The existence of Seymour Kinnin-tucky was wiped off the face of the earth."

"Not entirely. There's still a record of your birth."

He dismissed the thought with a wave of his hand. "I don't exist except as a manatee. Right now, I'm trapped in a world where I don't belong."

If he wanted her to feel pity, it was working.

"Did you have any children with Lubblubb. Was that, um, even possible?"

"Yes, it was possible. I was a manatee through and through. We had three calves. Two of them are bulls now with their own families. A boat killed the third when she was young."

"I'm so sorry. Did your other two children stay in touch?"

"Remember, we're animals. We don't get together for the holidays. But our two bulls are in this general area. I've seen them from time to time."

Missy yawned. "I'm going back to bed. I need more sleep before I go to work tonight."

"You know, I'm very grateful for you taking me in like this," Seymour said. "I tell you what: I'll make you dinner before you leave for work."

"How?"

He laughed. "My memories of being a human have been coming back to me. Like how to cook. I'll rustle up something special for you from whatever's on hand."

"I look forward to that."

She most definitely did not.

THE FIRST WARNING sign was the lit candles on the dining room table. They weren't her formal candlesticks. Instead, he had found the tea candles she used when casting spells. They had a strong burning-tire scent, which wasn't ideal at the dinner table. The second warning sign was the music. Having spent the last few decades as a manatee, Seymour knew nothing about digital music. He did, however, manage to tune the radio to a country music station. Candles plus music equaled not the kind of dinner she wanted to have with him.

"I found a bottle of white wine in the fridge," he said. "Would you care for some?"

"No thanks. I'm going to work after this."

"Yes, of course. I just wanted to set the right mood."

"We don't need a mood," Missy said. "We just need a meal."

"Then I'll serve."

Missy sat at the table. There was no silverware on it. Seymour exited the kitchen carrying two large plates covered with what appeared to be salads. He placed one in front of her.

It held half a head of iceberg lettuce, sliced carrots and apples, green olives, pickles, slices of Swiss cheese, half an uncooked eggplant, croutons, and potato chips. Atop it lay sprigs of something she couldn't identify. It looked like rosemary but wasn't.

He sat down with his plate across from her.

"I created this with items on hand. For you."

He gazed at her intensely, then twitched his eyebrows. He had very bushy eyebrows.

He reached to his plate with both hands and began shoving food into his mouth, chewing loudly and allowing food debris to tumble from his lips to his lap. He arched a bushy eyebrow at her as if to ask why she wasn't eating.

Missy nibbled on a piece of carrot.

"What's this?" she asked, holding up the unidentified green.

"Hydrilla," he said with his mouth full. "From the canal."

Her appetite evaporated. But she forced herself to eat more carrot and some apple. She looked at her watch and figured she could find an excuse for leaving for work early.

"Manatees don't normally form bonded pairs like Lubblubb and me," Seymour said, crunching on a carrot. "When a cow goes into heat, she has a herd of bulls following her around, trying to mate with her. Maybe it's because I was born human, but I was different. I stayed with Lubblubb year-round, not just when she was in heat. I had to fight off the other bulls during mating season and protect her. I wanted you to know that."

"That's . . . lovely," Missy said unconvincingly.

He continued to stare at her.

"You know, it's that time of year," he said.

"What time?"

"Mating season. Short but sweet, intense and memorable."

She shot up from her chair so fast it fell over.

"Thank you so much for a lovely meal," she said. "But I must be going. I have some difficult patients tonight."

"I'll see you when you return."

"Don't stay up for me. I'll be very late."

"How could I not stay up for you? Like I told you, I'm a protective bull, forever loyal."

She grabbed her tote bag and hurried from the house. They had to solve the mystery of the poisonings fast, especially the part about getting him to shift back to manatee. And stay that way.

She was anxious throughout her entire shift, worried that Seymour was going to make advances at her in the future. She had hoped he wouldn't be attracted to human females. She was wrong. The human genes he was born with seemed to have left their mark.

She returned home at 4:10 a.m. The light on the front porch

was burning, but the house was dark and quiet. Letting herself in the front door, the lamp on the table in the foyer was on, as it should be. A dim light came from the kitchen, probably from the range hood. All was quiet. She could slip undetected into her bedroom except for one problem: the cats.

Both showed up as if out of nowhere, rubbing against her legs. They wanted to be fed.

She tiptoed into the kitchen with cats in tow. She grabbed two small plates from a cabinet and a can of wet food from the pantry. Both cats jumped onto the counter to supervise. She popped the tab and pulled the can open.

Cra-a-a-ck went the aluminum.

"You have returned, my lovely cow."

Seymour stood in the doorway to the kitchen. He was naked except for a hibiscus flower clenched in his teeth that he must have taken from the bush in the backyard.

"Seymour, word to the wise: Human women don't like to be called cows. Unless you want a broken nose."

Missy's words didn't seem to faze him.

"How can a silly word define you? Your fecundity is all that matters."

She kept her eyes off his ample belly, which fortunately blocked her vision of his privates. His man-breasts sagged, as did his jowls. She had no issue with heavy men, but this dude used to be a manatee. In fact, he was probably more attractive in manatee form than this.

"Let me set some ground rules," Missy said. "As long as you're staying in my home, you will wear clothes at all times. The only exception being when you wash yourself behind the closed and locked door of the guest bathroom. And you will not leave this house unless you are clothed. Lastly, and most importantly, I am not in heat. I am not fecund. I am not waiting for a herd of manatee bulls to chase me around the river. I am middle-aged, about to begin menopause. I will have no romantic interest in any man whom I haven't grown to know and love over a long period of time. Your charms, though considerable, considerably sizable, are not interesting to me. Do you understand?"

The hibiscus flower dropped from his mouth. His face reddened.

"Don't take it personally, Seymour. I'm sure you're a most attractive bull underwater. But I'm focused right now on stopping the killing of manatees. And you should be, too."

"Of course, I am," he said in a weak voice.

"And you're not exactly a young bull anymore. Get your mind out of your groin and stop acting like a dirty old man. It's not becoming."

"Message received," he said. He retreated to the guest bedroom, his sagging buttocks jiggling.

But then he stopped.

"Should you ever reconsider, you know where to find me!"

8

VAMPIRE DIPLOMACY

The house was in one of the oldest residential neighborhoods of Jellyfish Beach, a couple of blocks from downtown, with structures from the late-nineteenth and early twentieth centuries. Many of the homes were charmingly restored and evoked the early pioneer period of this part of Florida. Some of them had been converted to office space.

This house, in the middle of the block, had been neglected. It looked like no one had occupied it for years. For vampires to live in a house that looked haunted was almost too on-the-nose. But from as far as a block away, Agnes felt the presence of the undead here.

"Oleg," she said, "park along the street up here. There are vampires in that yellow house on the right."

It was a two-story, Mediterranean style with a barrel-tile roof, arched windows, and stucco walls, from the 1920s. Twin concrete wheel paths led to a detached garage just big enough to hold a Ford Model A.

"I sense several vampires inside," Sol said.

It wasn't long after sunset in the time of year when the sun set early. The vampires inside would be up, but it wasn't late enough to go hunting. The downtown area was still bustling with diners and partiers. In an area like this, you needed to wait until closing time when you could pick off lone stragglers wandering the darkened streets.

An abandoned baby carriage sat in the front yard that someone had turned into a planter. The plants were all dead. The upstairs windows were shuttered. One of the downstairs windows was missing a pane. The front yard was mostly weeds, with beer cans and an empty plastic bag blown up against an out-of-control ficus hedge that was growing past the bottom of the windows.

"I don't have a good feeling about this," Bill said. "Should we bring stakes with us?"

"No. They'll think we're attacking," Oleg said as he parked the minivan filled with vampires along the curb.

"All we need to do is introduce ourselves and leave a number where they can reach us," Agnes said.

The other night, when they had met with the members of the Alligator Hammock HOA, it had been a delight. The gated community west of town for residents fifty-five and older (in body age) was inhabited by retired senior vampires like themselves. The men and women of the board were friendly and eager to set up an alliance with Squid Tower to provide mutual support in the face of threats against vampires. In fact, they also promised to arrange a pickleball tournament between the two communities.

Agnes wasn't optimistic about the vampires in this house.

The four of them exited the minivan and trudged up a cracked concrete walkway to the front door. Agnes tried the doorbell. It didn't work. She rapped on the front door with the handle of her quad cane.

A large, heavyset vampire wearing a purple velvet smoking jacket opened the door. His jet-black hair was molded into a pompadour, and his puffy, middle-aged face appeared to be wearing makeup. He smiled, not bothering to retract his fangs.

"Welcome," he said. "New vampires in town?"

"We've lived on the beach forever," Agnes said. "In Squid Tower."

"Oh, at last we meet. It's well known that vampires aren't allowed to hunt near your territory. I rarely go to the beach at all except to pluck a few tasty vagrants from the public beach before dawn now and then."

"I'm Agnes. This is Oleg, Bill, and Sol."

"I'm Enrico."

"We're trying to organize the vampires of Jellyfish Beach into an informal cooperation agreement. It's in case there's ever a threat against us. A clan of hostile vampires tried to take over the town recently."

"Yes, I heard about that. Quite distasteful."

"They almost staked me," Oleg said.

Enrico shuddered. "I'm sorry to hear that. Will you come inside and meet the rest of our little hive?"

"Thank you," Agnes said, though she still felt uneasy.

Enrico led them through a formal foyer into a parlor facing the street. The house was just as decrepit within as without. There was water damage on the walls and ceilings with patches of black mold. The parlor held a couch covered with a dirty pink sheet and two wobbly dining room chairs. The floor was littered with used hypodermic needles. An empty liquor bottle stood beside the couch.

Agnes realized a young vampire woman sat on the floor in a corner, half covered by the dusty drapes.

"This is Maria," Enrico said. "She recently joined us. We're teaching her how to feed on humans. Another member of our hive, Sylvia, brought her to us. Maria was turned quite recently, and her maker was killed. Her maker was one of the vampires who wanted to take over the town."

He gave a knowing look. Agnes' pulse quickened. Hopefully, the young woman wouldn't associate Squid Tower with the demise of her maker.

"We give drugs to runaways and young people who drop out of recovery centers," Enrico said. "That's our most dependable source of prey. Maria is learning the hard way not to feed on drug addicts right after they were using."

He canted his head in her direction and smirked as she lolled on the floor in a stupor.

Two vampires entered the room from another doorway. One was a short, stocky African-American man with graying hair cut short. The other was a Caucasian man in his twenties with a shaved head and a giant blond bushy beard. He had a swastika tattooed on his head.

"This is John and Billy Ray. John moved to Jellyfish Beach from the Bahamas in the late eighteen hundreds and he never left. Billy Ray is a kid in comparison. He was turned only thirty years ago. Everyone, meet the adorable vampires from Squid Tower."

"We wanted to introduce ourselves," Agnes said. "We vampires need to stick together in case there are threats from outsiders," she glanced at Maria, who seemed too out of it to be listening. "And threats from within our city. Such as the police who take it upon themselves to extrajudicially execute vampires."

"What's that 'extra' word?" Billy Ray asked.

"When cops decide to stake you on the spot without an arrest or trial," Enrico said. "I've told you there are cops who know about vampires. They're our biggest threat."

Agnes knew these vampires were tempting fate by having drugs in the house.

"I know they's a threat," Billy Ray said. "That's why I keep 'em tied up!" He laughed.

"What do you mean?" Agnes asked with dread.

"I'll show you. C'mon."

Billy Ray led Agnes and her companions through a dining room where a man in a business suit lay sleeping on the table, through a butler's pantry, and into a kitchen that hadn't been used for cooking food in decades.

A young African-American man sat tied to a chair near a window boarded up with plywood. His mouth was covered by duct tape. He looked at them with eyes open with fear.

"He come poking by here last night, pretending to be a druggie. He's a narc. I haven't decided if I want to drain him dry or keep him around as my blood supply for a few more days."

This was very dangerous, Agnes thought.

"You are being unwise," Oleg said. "If you kill this detective, the police will stake every last one of you."

Oleg spoke with the authority of a former military officer. But the vampire skinhead wasn't buying it.

"How are they going to stake us? We're faster than them, stronger than them, and their bullets can't kill us."

"Yes, they can stake you. I've seen it happen."

The skinhead laughed, "Whatever, old man."

"I'm old in body age, but I've also been a vampire for over two hundred years. I've learned a lot. I know that imbeciles like you don't last very long as vampires."

"I didn't ask you to come to our house. You barged in and now you're insulting me."

"I am very good at mesmerizing humans," Agnes said. "I'll wipe his entire memory of this house away. You can let him go, and it will be like nothing happened."

Enrico entered the kitchen.

"Do as she suggests, Billy Ray," he said. "I own this house, and I'm the leader of this hive."

John came up beside Enrico in a show of support.

"Don't endanger us all," he said in a Bahamian accent.

"I killed a cop when I was human, and I got away with it," Billy Ray said defiantly.

"Because you were lucky, pure and simple," Enrico said. "Vampires survive on wit and wisdom, not luck. The gift of immortality is too great to depend on cheap luck."

"You're so full of yourself. Free the dang cop, I don't care. But if he returns another time to arrest us for drugs, that's gonna be on you. Vampires don't do so good in jail."

Billy Ray stomped out of the room.

"Thank you for talking sense to him," Enrico said. "I rarely come into this room. I didn't know the cop was here."

"This isn't just dangerous for you," Agnes said, "but for all vampires in Jellyfish Beach. Perhaps I'm risk-adverse because I'm a senior, but I've existed for over fifteen hundred years, and I don't want to jeopardize that."

"Giving drugs to your prey isn't the smartest thing, either," Sol said.

"Did you nice people come here to band together with us or to be the morality police?" Enrico asked.

"He's right, Sol," Agnes said. "I happen to agree with you, but their hunting techniques are none of our business."

The undercover detective whined to get their attention. He

had heard that his freedom might be imminent. If the vampires didn't change their minds.

"Let's get him out of here," Enrico said to John. "I will take you up on your offer to mesmerize him, Agnes. It sounds as if you can do it much more thoroughly than I."

"We have to get him out of the house and out of this neighborhood. After I mesmerize him, he'll forget everything before that point, but not afterward. Oleg, Sol, and Bill—help them put him in the minivan."

They complied without asking questions. They knew what they needed to do.

The three vampires plus John untied the detective from the chair, but kept his wrists bound and mouth covered. They half-carried, half-walked him outside and into the middle seat of the minivan.

"We'll take it from here," Agnes said to Enrico and John. She handed them her calling card. "Do stay in touch."

Oleg drove with Agnes riding shotgun and the prisoner sitting between Sol and Bill. They went to a public park along the Intracoastal they could enter despite the late hour. After parking, they took the cop as discretely as possible to a bench facing the water and sat him on it.

They untied his wrists and tore the tape from his mouth as Agnes simultaneously locked her eyes with his. He went limp.

"You will forget everything and all things regarding the house on Stork Street and its residents. And everything that happened to you there and tonight."

She waved her hand and walked away. The detective would be completely amnesic and in a foggy mental state for an hour or more before his basic memories returned.

If he happened to turn his head and see the vampires walking away, he wouldn't remember it. If, by chance, he did, the memory would be of a group of elderly citizens on a stroll. A very unremarkable sight in Jellyfish Beach.

Once they drove away, Agnes said to the others, "that young woman Enrico took in, the one intoxicated by the drug-laden blood she fed upon: If she was one of the humans the Neanderthal vampires received from the drug-recovery company, we can't let her stay in that house. She's a recovering addict. That's too dangerous for her."

"Can a vampire overdose and die?" Sol asked.

"To be quite frank, I don't know. Drugs are such a recent phenomenon."

9

TROUBLE BREWING

Matt was on a mission. Ever since Missy found no signs of magic at the Barbarian Boat Works factory, he was determined to discover where the potion was being created and distributed. Learning that a boat caught dumping a substance into the Intracoastal was registered to the company was enough to turn him into a pit bull that just wouldn't let go. The company was involved in this somehow, and they were the only lead he and Missy had. The company could be the ones making the potion, or maybe only warehousing and shipping it, but he knew for sure they were dumping it.

He searched public records and found the company owned a small warehouse along a railroad siding not far from their factory. He excitedly told Missy and drove her to the building after business hours. It was one of several identical, nondescript structures along the tracks. Mindful of security cameras, they pulled up to the building with his car's license plate not facing the building.

Missy did her magick thing for about five minutes and announced that she couldn't detect any black magic on the property. Another miss. He wondered if the boat company rented, rather than owned, space they could use for making the potion. But commercial leases weren't public records. He didn't know how he could find this out. Only a detective armed with a warrant could pull that off.

"I'm stumped," Matt said to Missy as they walked into The Ripped Tide for beers after they struck out at the warehouse.

"Me, too," Missy said. "It's one thing to find a polluter who's doing it to save money. It's quite another to find someone who's doing it deliberately to kill manatees. Why would anyone want to do that?"

They sat at a battered wooden table near a window with a view of the dumpster. It was the nicest table in this establishment, which attracted surfers, bikers, and others who were serious about drinking and not about ambiance.

"Whaddaya want?" asked a heavily tattooed server.

"Oh, hi Jane," Matt said. "Congratulations on your acquittal."

"The jury decided the bum had it coming to him."

"Well, God rest his evil soul," Matt said. "Two pints of Crabby Lager, please."

"Nope. We ain't got that anymore. Crabby Brewing went out of business a couple of months ago."

"They did? I hadn't heard. That's really sad. I used to buy beer to go at their brewery all the time. I'll miss them."

"Then whaddaya want instead?"

"Another craft beer. Surprise us."

When the server walked away, Missy said, "never ask a place like this to surprise you."

"Good point. Man, I'm disappointed about Crabby Brewing. They had a cool facility. All the tanks and stuff visible to the public when you went there. I'm passionate about beer. Speaking of passion, how's your roommate doing?"

Missy gave him a dirty look. "Fine."

"Has he been behaving?"

"He's overstaying his welcome."

Matt was happy to hear that. He didn't want to admit he was jealous, but a strange man living in Missy's home really bothered him.

Missy steered the conversation away from manatees and made small talk about her work. One of her werewolf patients had a case of worms, and the only medication she could find for it was made for dogs.

Then an interesting idea crept into Matt's head.

"You know, I was thinking about the brewery," he said.

"Instead of listening to me?"

"Isn't that how it works? Women talk, and men don't listen."

"Do you understand now why I prefer being single?"

He heard that. And didn't like it. But he went on to explain his idea.

"A vacant brewery, with an ample water supply, all sorts of tanks and valves, good drainage. Wouldn't that be a great place if you needed to create hundreds or even thousands of gallons of a particular liquid?"

Missy stared at him in rapt attention.

"You're right," she said, "it would be."

"It's a real long shot, but maybe I should search property records and see if anyone bought the brewery."

"Maybe you should."

His laptop was in his messenger bag and, believe it or not, The Ripped Tide had Wi-Fi. In a few minutes, he had an answer.

"An entity named Floss Enterprises bought the brewery last month. Let me see if I can find out anything about them."

Two beers later, after scouring public records, newspaper archives, business registries, and the far reaches of the internet, Matt found nothing.

"I think they're a shell company to disguise who the real owners are," he said.

"What should we do?"

"Keep an eye on the brewery. It's probably going to be remodeled and turned into another establishment. But you never know."

MATT WOULD HAVE LOVED to stake out the brewery with Missy, but because of their opposite work schedules, they split the duty. Missy put in some hours before and after work, as did Matt. They couldn't cover the place twenty-four hours a day, but they were there often enough to give them a good chance of seeing if anything was going on.

Matt showed up one night around 7:00 p.m. and was surprised to see the building had its lights on and three cars behind it. He parked on the street, away from any streetlamps, but close enough to see the brewery.

Two hours went by. He was hungry and bored. But then headlights swept the road, and a car left the property. It was an old Chevy, but he couldn't tell who was in it. So that meant two cars were still there.

He waited another hour, and just when he considered leaving to find a bathroom, a rental box truck rumbled down the road and parked behind the brewery.

Now this was getting interesting.

Thirty minutes later, the truck left the property. Matt listened to his hunch to follow the truck. It drove away from the neighborhood of warehouses and light industry, then turned west onto a main road. A little later, it entered the northbound ramp for the interstate highway. Matt followed. This was so exciting he forgot he had to pee.

Matt called Missy to update her on the developments. She didn't answer, probably because she was with a patient, so he left a long voicemail.

Who knows where the truck was going? At least at this late hour, the traffic on the highway was thin and Matt easily stayed with the truck even at a safe distance.

After traveling for about an hour, the truck exited and turned on the first road east. Almost immediately, it pulled into a public park with a boat ramp on an oxbow of a river. Matt killed his headlights and entered the park, stopping just inside the entrance.

The truck reversed toward the boat ramp. A center-console motorboat idled at the end of a pier beside the ramp. The park had enough lighting that Matt had no trouble seeing a man ride the hydraulic lift at the truck's tailgate as it lowered to the concrete. Three plastic drums rode with him. When it touched the ground, he rolled them one by one down the pier and two men in the boat helped lower them onto its deck.

Matt was too far away to see the registration number on the boat's hull, but he wrote down the license plate of the truck and its USDOT number outside the driver's door.

The boat sped away. The man closed the rear of the truck and climbed into the passenger seat of the cab. Since Matt couldn't follow the boat, he followed the truck which got back on the interstate headed north. It must have more deliveries to make.

After another forty minutes of driving, the truck exited again and headed east. The trip east was much longer this time. Finally, as the road rose to a bridge over the Intracoastal, the truck turned right at an intersection and soon came to a boat ramp park. Here, the process repeated, with a large commercial fishing boat receiving five drums.

After watching the delivery, Matt called Missy and left another message. He slipped out of the car to relieve himself in some trees. He couldn't have waited any longer.

The truck restarted its engine. Matt forced himself to finish. He zipped up, turned around.

The impact to his skull created an explosion of light behind his eyes before everything went black.

10

SNOOPING

M issy noticed she had a voice message after seeing a vampire from Poughkeepsie with a peptic ulcer and Leonard Schwartz, who had a foul disposition no matter how healthy he was.

She was amazed to learn that the out-of-left-field theory of the brewery being used to make the potion turned out to be true. Matt left additional messages about the deliveries of barrels to two boats at two different waterways. But that was it. No more messages. She tried calling him and went straight to voice mail and asked him to call her.

At the back of her mind was a nagging feeling of dread. But maybe she was just being paranoid.

She planned to do some digging into the brewery. If a shell company was used to purchase it, surely there must be a way to find out the real owners. When Matt returned her call, they could devise a plan.

In the meantime, she had other problems to deal with. A horny shifter, for one. When she returned home, she found a hibiscus flower on her pillow. That might have been romantic if a husband or lover had left it there. Not when a middle-aged mer-manatee without a job invaded her personal space to do it.

And then on the local news was a story about more manatee deaths. Some had beached themselves before dying, and others washed up dead in the St. Lucie River. The story mentioned that additional deaths were recorded in Vero Beach.

She did a news search on the internet and found deaths occurring all across the state. This was serious. Now that she knew about the black magic, she feared for the worst.

It was apparent that someone was trying to wipe out manatees in Florida.

Were Matt, Seymour, and she the only ones who knew and cared?

She looked up websites of organizations that were dedicated to saving manatees. Fortunately, there were many. But they lacked the clout to change laws and regulations. And they surely didn't realize someone with black magic was coming for their sea cows.

She emailed the directors of the largest organizations, explaining that she and a reporter were investigating the recent mysterious deaths of manatees. They had reason to believe that it was a deliberate, coordinated attempt to poison the creatures. She recommended that they alert their members to keep an eye out at locations where manatees lived. Look for boats carrying large plastic drums.

One director emailed her back later and seemed to believe her. She promised Missy the Mothers for Manatees would be vigilant.

"Our members are very passionate and hands-on when it comes to rescuing and protecting our beloved manatees," the woman wrote. "If we catch any bad actors, we will kick their butts!"

Every effort will help, Missy tried to believe.

She tried calling Matt again. No answer. She drove to his apartment in the dim light of early morning. He lived in a small bungalow near downtown. His car wasn't there, and no one answered the door. She saw no signs of a break-in at the bungalow.

She considered calling the police and filing a missing-persons report. Right now, that seemed premature and a bit desperate. She needed to know where he had been last, before he disappeared.

One of Matt's fishing poles leaned against the door frame on his back porch. The long rod had a lure tied on that Matt liked to cast into the surf, occasionally catching bluefish, jack crevalle, and snook. He was fond of this rig, so she took it with her to use in a magick spell to find him.

There was little else she could do now but wait. And she refused to do that.

She returned home. Fortunately, Seymour wasn't there. He'd been going to the municipal pool to do laps each day to regain strength, hoping it would help him recover his ability to shift. He also realized that blubber didn't look as flattering on a middle-aged human as it did on a manatee bull. So Missy had the house to herself.

She drew a large magick circle on her kitchen floor, large enough to hold her and the fishing rod. First, she would do a locator spell. It was a vision-based spell that had its drawbacks, but it was a good idea for beginning a search when you didn't know where to look.

She cleared her mind and drew upon the energies within her and from the earth. She said a short invocation and felt the power light up her mind. First, she sent out tracer spells, tiny balls of magick. They fanned out across the landscape like a swarm of drones. They relied on visual matches and weren't as effective in finding a person who might be indoors, but pretty good at locating vehicles and such. She sent them looking for Matt's pickup truck. His voice messages said that he went north on the interstate, but she sent the tracer spells in other directions as well, just in case.

She waited, her mind blank, her senses alert. Several minutes passed.

Her mind lit up as a tracer pinged her. A vision formed of Matt's old truck parked at a boat ramp park at the edge of a wide stretch of the Intracoastal Waterway.

Maintaining the image in her head, she grasped the power charm in her pocket and said a more powerful locator spell to find out where this park was. Soon, the view of his truck in the parking lot zoomed out until it was like looking at a satellite view of an internet map.

She recognized the location as being near Vero Beach. She allowed the spells to fade.

Now that she knew where he had been abducted, she would attempt to find him. That's where the fishing pole came in. As a cherished possession that he frequently touched, it held a residue of his psychic energy, almost like fingerprints.

She drew in more energies to cast the next spell, a more powerful one. She recited cryptic words in Old English, grasping the power charm in her left hand and the handle of the fishing rod in her right.

She sent a surge of energy through her arm and into the rod, uttering the last words of the invocation.

A glowing orb appeared, floating in the air above the fishing rod. It was born from Matt's psychic energy in the rod, and it naturally sought to join again with the center of Matt's energy —within Matt himself.

"Go forth and find him," she commanded the ball, "find Matt Rosen and be as one again."

The orb zipped away from her and passed through the kitchen wall. But before it did, she had created a mental connection with it.

The wait wasn't long before a vision flooded her head: Matt, in the cab of a truck, his wrists and ankles bound with zip ties. He slumped against the seat, dried blood caked in his hair. A beefy looking guy with a shaved head was in the seat to his right, playing with his phone. To his left was the driver, a dark guy with a beard. The truck was a common box type with a rental company logo. They were cruising on a highway.

Missy commanded the orb to leave the cab and remain above it, so she could see the highway signs and figure out where they were.

Soon, she got her answer. They were on State Road 528, headed west toward Orlando.

Unfortunately, she couldn't maintain the spell long enough to find out where they were taking Matt. That could take hours. No witch had enough stamina to make a powerful spell like this last so long. She would have to try again later.

She broke the connection and ended the spell, collapsing on the floor with exhaustion. She crawled from the magic circle and found her phone to call the police, but hesitated. How was she going to explain that she saw him in the truck with his hands and feet bound? She would have to concoct an elaborate lie about witnessing his kidnapping. She would have to do it anonymously.

"Hello, what is the nature of your emergency?"

"I saw a man violently abducted. They took him in a

Discount Rentals truck on 528 headed toward Orlando. I last saw them at mile marker 24."

She hung up. Would they take her call seriously? If she could find out where they were bringing him, she could call the Orlando police, and it wouldn't be difficult for them to check it out.

She painfully got off the floor. It was important to regain her strength. She had snooping to do.

BY LATE MORNING, she was at the brewery, relieved to find the parking lot empty. But she didn't park there just yet. She needed to get a little magick out of the way.

She drove slowly down the street past an office park as she assembled the spell. Doing a U-turn, she drove back to the brewery. She didn't stop where security cameras could capture an image. She rolled past, as if she had business elsewhere on this street. When she was in front of the brewery, she let loose a quick burst of magnetic energy designed to knock the cameras off their internet connection and fry their backup memory cards.

Now, she could park safely in the lot, in a place where her car wouldn't be seen from the street. As she walked toward the building, she devised a similar spell, this time to disarm the alarm system.

Don't get the wrong idea: Missy was not a burglar. She was coming up with these magick tactics on the fly. She wasn't entirely sure they would work.

The lock on the main entrance wasn't fancy, just a standard deadbolt. It didn't take long for her magick to engage the cylinders and snap it open. She held her breath and opened the door.

The alarm didn't sound, thank heavens.

The inside of the brewery was filled with shadows and chaos. Her spell to disable the alarm had also knocked the power out, so she relied on a flashlight and the small amount of light that streamed in a row of clerestory windows beneath the ceiling.

She walked into a bar-restaurant area, but all the tables had been moved to accommodate dozens of empty white plastic barrels. The brewing equipment was visible through a wall of glass at the rear of the room. Stainless steel tanks in various sizes and shapes, dense rows of pipes, and clusters of valves and gauges. It meant nothing to her. What was important were the sacks of spices piled in a corner of the room. Several were labeled as nutmeg, but there were also sacks of cinnamon, ginger, allspice, and cloves.

The black magic was unmistakable in the air. Its presence was fresh and strong. Just like an individual portion of the potion would be made in a sorcerer's kitchen or lab, the ingredients would be added to the water in a certain order, mixed well, then heated. The black magic spell would be applied at different stages, with the main blast given to the potion at the end of the process.

Missy couldn't imagine how much power and energy it must take to enchant several fifty-gallon drums.

Satisfied she'd found the source of the deadly potion, she searched for any incriminating paperwork in the building. A photocopy of the potion recipe was taped to the wall in the brew room. She removed it and put it in her pocket. She wanted an invoice or work order. Or simply a name somewhere. But the culprits had been careful to leave no hard copies of their communications.

It was time to go. Now that she was guilty of breaking and

entering, she briefly thought about committing arson, too—burning the place down. But property destruction and violence were against her magick code, except when absolutely necessary for self-defense. And it would only delay, not stop, the manatee killers. She would love to see them all arrested, but there wasn't anything illegal going on in this building. She would need to find out who was killing the manatees and prove it.

The most important thing was to stop the magician behind this potion. How she would do that, she had no idea.

She exited the building and reversed her unlocking spell to lock the door. She didn't bother trying to re-arm the alarm system because she wasn't sure how, and it might go off while she was still on the property.

As she walked to her car, a pickup truck and SUV entered the parking lot. She picked up her pace.

"Hey, what are you doing here?" a bearded man shouted from the SUV's open window.

She ignored him, got in her car, and drove out of the lot before they could think of blocking her in. But they had seen her and her car. This could be a big problem.

They didn't appear to follow her, so she drove home. She wanted to do another locator spell to see where Matt was. If she could determine an exact location, then she could call the police and let them know.

She parked in the driveway and went inside. Seymour hadn't returned yet. It was past her bedtime, and she was exhausted, but she needed to locate Matt. First, a cup of black tea for the caffeine.

Actually, first the cats must be fed. Rubbing against her legs and meowing, they made perfectly clear what her chief priority was. After she opened cans of wet food and presented the plates to the cats like she was a server in a high-end restaurant, she set about brewing some tea.

While the water boiled, she checked her email. There was a second response from a manatee organization. This one was dubious about her claims and encouraged her to make a donation, fully tax deductible! She sighed and deleted it.

The kettle whistled, and she poured the boiling water into her cup with the tea bag. She rarely bothered with loose tea, because she sometimes got it mixed up with her magick ingredients. Once she accidentally made a cup of tea from ground hemlock bark. Not a pleasant experience.

She sat down to enjoy her tea.

And then the back door exploded inward.

BREAKING AND ENTERING

The man with the beard burst through the back door into the kitchen, glanced around and saw her. He was the one who had confronted her at the brewery.

"You've been very naughty," he said, striding up to her.

She flung her hot tea in his face and ran. Like her cats, she ran to her bedroom. And, like the cats, she hadn't done any strategic thinking and put herself into a dead end.

She locked the door and began casting a warding off spell to drive the man from her house.

Her bedroom door crashed open, a piece of the frame flying onto her bed.

So much for the warding spell.

"Why are you being so unfriendly?" the man asked with a leer. "I just want to ask you some questions."

She was too busy casting a protection spell to answer.

He approached her. She backed up against the wall.

"We saw you leaving the brewery. Why were you there?"

"I heard the building was on the market," she said.

Concentrate on the spell, she reminded herself.

"It's not on the market," the man said, looking around the room. "It's not smart to go snooping around other people's business. Like your friend did. My associates caught him spying on them."

She didn't answer. She tried to activate her spell, but her racing heart and pounding temples weren't making it easy.

"Who are you working for?" he asked. "Mothers for Manatees?"

When she didn't answer, he walked over to the bed, reached under it, and came out with a yowling cat. It was Brenda. He held her by the scruff of her neck.

"Answer me or I break the cat's neck."

This was beyond the pale. Her surging anger was greater than her fear now.

She closed her eyes, chanted an invocation with the power charm in her hand, and the man screamed.

Brenda dropped to the ground and raced from the room.

The man held his right hand gingerly before him.

"What did you do?"

"Nothing," she lied. "Must have been static electricity from the cat's fur."

She ran for the door. He grabbed her hair and pulled her back. She swung around and kicked him in the family jewels. That gave her a moment to escape the room.

She almost made it to the front door when he tackled her from behind. They landed on the hardwood floor, his weight atop her, pain flaring through her knees and shoulder where they hit the floor.

"You're going to regret that," he growled.

He dragged her by the arms into the kitchen, threw her onto the floor, and left her gasping for air. He picked up the toaster oven.

He's going to beat me with a toaster over? she wondered.

No, he yanked the electrical cord so hard it came free from the appliance, wires dangling, and he tied her arms behind her back with it.

He pulled his phone from his pocket. Breathing heavily, he scrolled, pressed the screen, and put the phone to his ear.

"I followed her home, and we had a little dust up," he said. "Yes, we're going to have a chat right now. Yeah, I'll use extreme tactics if I need to." He looked at her to assure himself that she heard this. "I'm sure she knows what's going on."

She heard the other voice, a male, but not what he was saying.

"Yeah, okay, but then what?"

He paced across the floor.

"Sure, I can do that. It wouldn't be my first. But where should I dispose of it afterwards?"

Dispose of it? Did he mean dispose of me?

"Yeah, I know where that is. I can do it there in daylight? Okay, okay, I'll let you know. Sure, that would be great. Order for me the quinoa and kale salad, dressing on the side."

He turned toward Missy and studied her coldly, like a piece of furniture that had to be dismantled.

"So you're with Mothers for Manatees, are you?" he asked.

She remained quiet.

"Are you going to answer me, or am I going to make life unpleasant for you?"

She stayed silent.

"Okay, It's your decision."

He took two steps backward, then toward her, swinging his leg back and slamming it forward in a soccer kick.

His foot bounced off her magick bubble and he stumbled forward, crushing into the kitchen table.

Her protection spell was up and working.

"What the heck happened?"

He came back at her and tried another kick. He got the same result.

"This makes no sense. What are you doing?"

"Get out of my house, and I won't do something very painful to you."

He smiled bitterly. "You're full of it."

He picked up a stool from the island counter and tried to hit her with it. It bounced off the bubble and he staggered backwards.

"This is insane," he said.

He threw the stool at her. It rebounded and hit him in the shins.

Missy was strict in her moral code about not using her magick for harm. Self-defense was the exception. Even so, she didn't have an armory of magick weapons. In fact, her type of magick didn't work that way. Black magic did, and that's why it was so frowned upon by witches and wizards.

Her magick could provide a few solutions, however.

Such as the spell she used next.

The man screamed as his hair was yanked upwards by an invisible force and he rose in the air, suspended six inches above the floor by his gel-saturated locks.

"Owww, what are you doing?"

"I told you to leave," she said. "Why are you still here?"

He pulled a handgun from the back of his pants.

Missy swallowed in fear. Her protection spell was potent, but could it withstand a bullet?

He pointed the gun at her head. She was about to find out. With no place to take cover, she willed more energy into the spell, hoping to strengthen it, and closed her eyes.

The gunshot was deafening, echoing in her kitchen. Ears ringing, she opened her eyes. She didn't feel like she was dead. Nothing hurt except where he had previously kicked and punched her.

A windowpane was shattered with a hole in it. The bullet must have ricocheted there.

He fired again with the same result. She didn't know how many bullets his clip held, but she added still more energy to her spell to keep it strong.

They seemed to have reached an impasse. He couldn't kill her, and she couldn't get him to leave. Perhaps she could use her magick and telekinesis to toss him out the door and then form a protection bubble around the house? No, she couldn't get the protection bubble up fast enough before he ran back inside.

"I'm going to kill you, I swear!" He said, his face red, spittle flying from his lips. "I'm going to— "

Seymour raced in the broken back door and tackled her assailant, smashing him into the island. The handgun went flying and landed at the base of the refrigerator.

Tufts of the man's hair, torn from his scalp, still hung suspended in the air.

Seymour grinned at Missy, then proceeded to demolish the bad guy with a flurry of punches to the head and stomach. He slammed the man face-down on the kitchen tile and locked his arms behind him in a law-enforcement hold.

"You're a lot more . . . aggressive than I thought for a manatee," Missy said.

"I told you I was in the military. I left out the part about being an Army Ranger."

"Oh, my."

"Why is he here?"

"He followed me home from the brewery. I'll explain more later." She didn't want the man to hear how much she knew.

"He's one of the guys killing the manatees?"

"Yeah."

Seymour gave the man another punch.

"That felt good," Seymour said. "What are we going to do with him? Chop him up and feed him to the fish?"

The man groaned.

"I'm calling the police," Missy said. "He broke in here and attacked me. I have the bruises to prove it. But before I call nine-one-one, I have a spell I'd like to try. Keep him secure and I'll be right back."

Missy stood up and headed for the garage where she kept her magick supplies. But first, she undid the spell that had lifted the man into the air. His torn-out hair, that had remained levitating by itself, dropped to the kitchen floor.

Many garages have work benches covered with tools and hardware. Missy's was for making charms and potions. So instead of boxes of nails and screws, she had jars of dried insects and strange herbs. In a small plastic container was a homemade powder she'd relied upon many times before.

She used the powder for her truth-telling spell, very simple but potent magick. It made the subject of the spell tell the truth willingly and eagerly, happy to cast off the burden of withheld information and correct deceit. The subject usually felt wonderful afterward, with a lighter conscience. That was before they realized they'd blurted out something that could have negative consequences.

Back when Missy was dating, after her husband divorced her and died, she used this spell on occasion. It was for the men she suspected didn't have good intentions. It turned out the spell always revealed that her instincts had been correct.

She returned to the kitchen. Seymour still had the bad guy in a hold on the floor, one that looked especially painful as the man struggled against him.

"Okay, Mr. Jerkface," Missy said, "I'm going to ask you a few questions, and you'll answer me truthfully."

"I'm not saying anything," he said in a muffled voice, his lips pressed to the tile.

"We'll see about that."

Missy sprinkled the powder upon the man, careful not to get any on Seymour. She then gathered her energies and recited the invocation in Latin, activating the spell.

"Who do you work for, Jerkface?" she asked.

"Manny."

"Who's Manny?"

"He's a fixer, an operative," the man said. "He does odd jobs for clients."

"Like killing manatees?"

"We just handle mixing the chemicals and arranging for them to be dumped in places where sea cows like to hang out."

"Why are you killing manatees?"

"Because they're a nuisance. They're bad for the economy, bad for the boat industry, bad for developers who want to build in their habitat."

"But why are you making them more endangered? That will just make the regulations stricter."

"Not if there aren't manatees at all anymore," the man said as if he were explaining it to a child.

"Are you serious? You're trying to make manatees extinct?"

"Well, in Florida anyway."

Missy had to pause for a moment to absorb the radical idea. It was both crude and evil.

"Why are you mixing the chemicals here in Jellyfish Beach?" she asked.

"Manny's client supplied the brewery here for us to use."

"Who is Manny's client?"

"Some political lawyer in Tallahassee."

"Who?"

"I don't have the name at the tip of my tongue."

Seymour twisted the man's arm. He yelped. Missy sprinkled more powder on the man's head and repeated the invocation. This guy was a hard case; she'd never had to double up on the spell before.

"Who is this lawyer?" she demanded.

"I don't know the guy's name. The firm is called the Apex Group."

"Why did you come here to kill me?"

"Manny said that we had to keep this operation absolutely secret. No one is supposed to learn about it. No one. If anyone finds out, they need to be eliminated."

"Wow," Seymour said.

"Who is your client's client?"

"Huh?"

"The guy who hired Manny is a lawyer. Someone hired him. Who was it?"

"Man, I don't know. I don't care. I just care about the sweet bonuses we're getting for this job."

Missy knew he was telling the truth. And it made her furious.

"Where is the reporter?" she demanded.

"What?"

"The reporter you kidnapped."

"I don't know what you're talking about."

"Your goons kidnapped a friend of mine at a boat ramp where the chemicals were loaded onto a boat. You said he was spying on them."

"I don't know where they took him," he said, his eyes looking at hers pleadingly, his resistance gone. "Honest. I just work in the brewery, loading up the product."

And assaulting women, she thought.

"Okay, we're almost done here," she said. "When is the next dumping of the barrels going to take place and where?"

"We're supposed to ship out the next batch tomorrow night. I don't know where's it going. They only tell the truck drivers the destination."

"One last question. Who is the black magician who puts the spell on the chemicals?"

"Spell? What are you talking about?" he asked, genuinely confused.

"Someone puts magic in the batches you make."

"I don't believe in magic."

"Have you seen anyone at the brewery who isn't part of your crew working for Manny?"

"There's this old lady who shows up every once in a while. I don't know why. Maybe she's the cleaning woman."

Oh-oh, Missy thought.

"What does she look like?"

"Really old, dyed jet-black hair, kinda short. She constantly chain smokes."

Mother, Missy realized. My mother who gave me away as an infant and tried to kill me as an adult. Mother, the black-magic sorceress who would do anything for a buck, is working for these guys?

It figured.

Missy broke the spell.

"I'm done with him," she said. "Hang onto him until the police get here."

"You know these guys are going to send someone else after you," Seymour said. "Good thing I'm staying here, so I can protect you."

Missy was suddenly even more motivated to take down the manatee killers, if only to get Seymour out of her house.

"Pay no attention to all that nonsense I was spouting off," the man said. "It was all lies."

"Unfortunately, it wasn't," Missy said.

After the police came and left with the thug in handcuffs, Seymour approached Missy.

"I want you to know something."

Uh-oh, she thought. I don't want to hear anything about love or mating.

"I didn't mean it when I suggested chopping up the guy and feeding him to the fish."

"I figured you were just trying to intimidate him. Plus, you wouldn't give your fish friends rotten meat."

"Right," Seymour said, "but what I want to make clear to you is I won't kill anymore."

"Anymore?"

"I was part of some serious action in Afghanistan. It got to the point I couldn't kill people anymore. So I retired from the Army at the end of my tour. But I still couldn't live with myself. That's part of why I shifted to a manatee permanently.

Manatees are peaceful, gentle creatures. I wanted to be one, too."

He held his intense emotions in check, but they affected Missy, too.

"I wanted you to know because while I promise to protect you, I won't kill anyone to do it. I can't."

"I would never expect you to kill for me," she said.

"Sometimes, really dangerous people leave you with no other option."

"Well, let's hope it never comes to that."

12

MOTHERS FOR MANATEES

The Crab County chapter of Mothers for Manatees split up its membership into teams, each assigned to a different boat ramp. The team at the Jellyfish Beach Intracoastal Park ramp spent several uneventful hours in a boat anchored near the ramp.

"What are the chances they come to our station tonight?" asked Mildred, a retired librarian from Boston. "Zilch."

Mildred was a gentle soul who loved all animals. She never imagined she would be sitting in a boat at night prepared to do battle to save her beloved manatees. But she had never before imagined that people would allegedly plot to poison them. There was something about being on a fixed income that made her empathetic for vulnerable creatures.

Mothers for Manatees was as far as one could get from an eco-terrorist group. But they did appreciate how important their image of being fighters was. Their foes were the powerful and the greedy who understood nothing except money and force. Mothers for Manatees didn't have the funding and the clout to shut down developers and polluters.

But they soon learned the crazier they acted, the more they were feared. Fear was their secret weapon.

"What are the chances they're only using boat ramps? Maybe they know a homeowner with a dock, and they load the boat there in privacy," suggested Tameka, a former bank executive who owned the boat they were on. She proudly wore on her left bicep a brand-new "M4M" tattoo that was styled as if it signified an outlaw biker gang. The recent manatee deaths, and the allegations that they were deliberate, brought out a militant side she hadn't known she had.

"Or maybe they use a waterfront restaurant that's closed for the evening," said Mee Ling who had led a lifelong crusade against bullies. "You know, like that one."

She pointed at a restaurant directly across the waterway from them. The lights of the parking lot behind the establishment revealed two men rolling large barrels around the side of the building and down an accessibility ramp to a waterfront deck. A large boat with its engine idling and its running lights turned off, was tied up there.

"We have to stop them," Mee Ling said.

"These punks need to learn a lesson," Tameka said, starting the boat's engine. "These waters don't belong to them."

"The waters belong to us!" Mildred said.

"No, they belong to the creatures that live in them."

"Oh. Right. Attack!" Mildred shouted. "Ramming speed! Prepare to board!"

Tameka started the boat while the others pulled up the anchor. She slammed down the throttle, and they crossed the channel at top speed.

Boris, a Russian most recently from New York's Brighton Beach, loved the Florida lifestyle. He especially loved boating. His small johnboat with an outboard engine was fine for fishing every weekend, but it couldn't compare to evenings like tonight when he was at the helm of a thirty-five-foot go-fast boat with 1,000-horsepower inboards.

It was thanks to his new job with Barbarian Boat Works. He loved it. He knew nothing about building boats, but that didn't matter as long as he did odd jobs with no questions asked. Many of them involved going offshore in the company's big racing boats with their monster engines to pick up plastic-wrapped packages from Bahamian freighters, then racing to shore at high speed, too fast for law enforcement to catch.

Less enjoyable were nights like this when he and two coworkers had to dump out the mysterious contents of fifty-gallon drums. All in all, he thought it was worth doing in return for living anonymously in the Witness Protection Program after testifying against his Russian mob bosses in New York. Considering all the blood he had on his hands over the years, this was a dream job. What could beat taking hot new boats at top speeds, even if he hit a manatee now and then?

But when he saw the center console outboard speeding directly at him, he had second thoughts. If the company's boat was wrecked, he'd lose his job. Finding another job would not be easy when his past was supposed to stay hidden.

The boat zipping across the channel had three old ladies aboard. And they were not slowing down. Were they crazy? Was this a suicide attack?

"Untie us!" he shouted.

Paulie and Alberto, who had been helping load the barrels, obeyed instantly when they saw the impending collision.

Boris gunned the engine, and as soon as the last line was free, shot forward. Let the old ladies hit the dock, he thought. It's their own fault.

But, somehow, they read his intentions and turned left to cut him off. He thought he could get past them just in time, but the other boat turned left again, right into his path. Boris swung the wheel right as soon as he cleared the restaurant's deck.

And slammed into the seawall. Paulie and Alberto flew into the water.

The old-lady pirate vessel, fenders dangling along its side, churned the water as its engine reversed, slowing the forward momentum. It drifted gently into the side of the thirty-footer, the fenders squishing between the two hulls.

"I'll take this chump," the oldest of the old ladies shouted. "You two go after the truck."

Boris stared in astonishment as the septuagenarian leaped onto his boat while her boat sped to the restaurant. Snarling, the blue-haired lady lunged at him. He tried to evade her, but she was too fast. She smacked him in the head with a fish club. She kept hitting him savagely until he dove off the side and joined Paulie and Alberto in the drink.

TAMEKA TIED her boat to the restaurant's deck. Mildred had taken control of the go-fast boat, knocking its captain with his rock-star blond hair into the water. But he and his crew members were swimming to freedom. Here on land, the other manatee killers were still rolling barrels from the truck, unaware that their delivery boat had departed. She and Mee

Ling charged up to the restaurant armed with a boat hook and a baseball bat.

An African-American man rolled a barrel from the truck to the accessibility ramp, where he waited for his coworker to help him roll it down the ramp without it escaping and rolling off the deck into the water.

"Excuse me, sir," Tameka said.

"Huh?"

"You really should seek medical attention for your concussion."

"What are you talking about?" he asked, right before being brained by a baseball bat.

He dropped to the ground next to the barrel.

His coworker, a skinny Caucasian dude with a nose ring, rolled a barrel toward the ramp. He halted when he saw his comrade unconscious on the ground.

The barrel rolled ahead without him and ran over his fallen comrade, bumping to a stop against a wooden piling.

"Is there a problem?" he asked the two senior women, his voice faltering.

Mee Ling nodded in the affirmative. Then swung her boat hook like a Major League hitter. The young manatee-killer took it in the back of his head, but managed to stay conscious and sprinted away from the deadly old ladies. He mounted the steps to climb into the truck's cab, but Tameka grabbed him by his long hair and yanked him to the ground.

"Why are you doing this?" she asked.

"Doing what?"

She kicked him in the leg. "Killing manatees."

"Killing manatees? I didn't realize that," he said, his voice quavering. "I thought we were just dumping bad beer or toxic waste. We're job creators."

She kicked him in the head.

"Manatees are a protected species and you're killing them. You should be ashamed of yourself."

"I am. I've been ashamed of myself since I was a little kid and I wet the bed."

"You'll make good of yourself now," Tameka said. "You put all these barrels back in your truck, and you take them back to where you got them. You tell those toxic polluters that if they kill any more manatees, they won't be creating any more jobs, they be creating license plates in state prison. You understand?"

He nodded frantically.

"Now get your butt up and put these barrels back on the truck."

"All by myself?"

"All by yourself, until your friend wakes up. If he wakes up before the police get here."

The young punk rolled the remaining barrels back to the truck, although he struggled to figure out how the hydraulic lift at the back of the truck worked.

Meanwhile, Mildred had piloted the bad guys' big cruiser back to the dock, and there were three fifty-gallon drums aboard that needed to be offloaded and rolled back up the accessibility ramp to the parking lot.

The young punk had three angry Mothers for Manatees to make sure he did it in short order.

The giant engine of the go-fast boat started up and roared as it sped away from the dock. The tall blond man was at the helm.

"I should have roughed him up more," Mildred said.

"It's okay," Mee Ling said. "he got our message."

13

THE WAGES OF AMORALITY

"**W**hat are these difficulties you mention?" Myron Hickey asked Manny Rodriguez, who had called him right before Myron's meeting with his biggest client.

"Nothing to be overly concerned with," Manny said. His tone was anxious, though. "There are indications that our work is no longer secret."

"Such as?"

"One of my guys got arrested."

"He got busted for dumping the chemicals?"

"No. For attacking a woman who was snooping in the facility where the chemicals are mixed."

"Who cares if she was snooping? It's a brewery. No one would know what they're putting in the barrels."

"This was right after we caught a guy spying on our crew delivering barrels to the boats. There had to be a connection."

"As long as it's not the EPA or the Fish and Wildlife Service, I'm not concerned," Myron said.

"Well, last night a distribution operation was broken up. A boat was damaged. One of Mr. Pistaulover's boats."

Now this was becoming more serious. Now Myron realized why Pistaulover had demanded the meeting he was about to walk into. He was actually grateful for Manny giving him the heads-up, so he didn't get ambushed.

"What exactly happened?" he asked.

"Mothers for Manatees. It was like a commando raid. The boat was being loaded at a waterfront restaurant after hours. The guys thought it would be safer to do it there rather than a public boat ramp after they caught that guy spying on them. It would have gone down flawlessly if those old ladies hadn't shown up. And then the police. The drivers got fined for trespassing and the shipment was confiscated."

"Confiscated?"

Myron was worried about this development. Now the Feds would get involved, wondering why they were dumping the barrels. The only thing that kept him from outright panic was the fact that the "chemical" mixture was technically harmless. The Feds could analyze it all they wanted and all they would find was nutmeg, cinnamon, and cloves. There was no way they'd know that black magic played a part in it.

The cover story he had devised for the operation was brilliant. The liquid in the drums was a special autumn beer that failed in the marketplace because everyone was sick of pumpkin pie spices. The brewery had sewer problems and couldn't dump enough of the beer there. So they'd had to improvise.

The problem with this story was the crews hired to dump it often got the story wrong. And it would be tricky trying to use this excuse if you were caught dumping the barrels into pristine natural springs upstate.

And the worst part of Myron's predicament was that the Feds would start keeping an eye on their operation. Maybe pumpkin-spice beer wasn't considered a toxic substance, at least by some, but there were laws against dumping stuff into the environment. Myron needed to look into that. Maybe he could lobby the legislature to pass a bill that gave an exception to pumpkin-spice beer.

"What do you want us to do?" Manny asked.

"Stick with the plan. The next manatee census is later this year. We're running out of time to kill manatees."

The door to the executive suite opened and an administrative assistant scurried out. Bob Pistaulover appeared in the doorway. Actually, his stomach appeared first, followed some time later by the rest of him. He had a shaved head and a permanent scowl. He carried himself like an ex-athlete who had let himself grow obese. The polo shirt with the Barbarian logo was as big as a circus tent but still clung tightly to his giant gut.

"Come in, Myron," he said.

The CEO of Barbarian Boat Works had a massive office that overlooked his manufacturing plant next door. The view was rows of newly built boats wrapped in plastic, lined up on the asphalt awaiting pickup by the trucks that delivered them to dealers all over Florida and the United States. Bob had an American flag over his desk and his office walls were covered with photos of his various bestselling boat models.

The guy lived in a $46-million mansion on the beach paid for by his profits. The profits he made even after spending a fortune on Myron's law firm.

"Great boating weather today, huh?" Myron said.

"Knock it off. One of my boats was damaged last night, attacked by some crazy environmentalists. I'm not letting you use my boats and drivers anymore. Find your own boats to use."

This wasn't a problem. That's what Myron's team did in other parts of the state. They used the Barbarian boats only because Pistaulover had volunteered them at the beginning of the manatee elimination program.

Pistaulover had also suggested that Myron purchase the brewery that had just come on the market. The CEO was deeply, personally vested in this project.

"I was told the crazy environmentalists that damaged my boat were the Mothers for Manatees. I'm going to sue them. I want to destroy those sea-cow huggers."

"Wait, Bob, not so fast. A lawsuit would bring horrible publicity for your company. A manufacturer of speedboats suing a non-profit run by sweet ladies trying to protect manatees? Not a good image for you. Plus, it connects you to the beer dumping."

Pistaulover sighed in frustration. Well, you have any better ideas to get these 'sweet ladies' off my back?"

Pistaulover was a notorious anti-environmentalist. His company had been fined millions over the years for dumping oils and acids into the river next to his factory. He was even more hostile to the environment than the real estate developers who were part of the coalition that hired Myron's firm. And that's saying something.

"I'll discredit them," Myron said. "Plant some fake news stories about misusing donations and make personal attacks against their board members. Don't worry, I'll make sure their fundraising dries up and their organization dies a slow death."

"I want it to be a fast death."

"Remember what I've told you about patience, Bob."

Pistaulover waved his beefy hand in disgust. Myron had heard the CEO not only hated the environment, but had a personal enmity against manatees. They were more than speed bumps to him. Something had happened to him in childhood that began his vendetta.

"Are these manatee women going to expose our operation?" Pistaulover asked.

"I wouldn't worry about that. But we need to step up the pace. Double our production of the potion and dump it in higher concentrations. Just in case word does get out, we don't want it to happen until it's too late to save the sea cows."

"Good. Are we capable of doubling production?"

"Sure, if we put more people on it."

"What about that witch or sorceress or whatever she is? Can she handle it?"

Pistaulover was the only member of the coalition who knew about the black magic. The other members didn't have a clue. Since the CEO had spearheaded the entire effort and micro-managed Myron every step of the way, it was impossible to keep the black magic secret from him.

Myron, who was proudly amoral, had used the sorceress before in his lobbying efforts. He wisely knew that she could help them kill manatees without a trace of toxins. Myron was surprised, though, that Pistaulover was okay with using black magic. The CEO was a big churchgoing man, or so he pretended. It seemed that profits won over moral scruples every time.

"I believe the witch can handle the increase in production. But she's going to raise her fee. And I'll need to charge more to cover the extra manpower."

"Go ahead. I have new models debuting next year. I want the manatee speed zones gone by then."

Myron thanked him, apologized for the damaged boat, and said goodbye. He was going to pay a visit to Manny in Orlando.

The little thug was beginning to screw up and needed an attitude adjustment.

And Myron wanted to talk to their prisoner. Find out how much the guy really knew about their operation. Before they killed him.

DURING HIS DRIVE TO ORLANDO, Myron wondered how he had messed up his Karma so badly in a previous life to deserve this assignment. And this assignment was going to stain his Karma even further.

He had been tasked with getting the West Indian manatee in the United States to lose its protection under the Endangered Species Act and the Marine Mammal Protection Act. Normally, this occurs when a species' population bounces back to a healthier level. That was not the case with manatees. He and others had helped down-list the species from "endangered" to "threatened," but manatee numbers were still low enough to keep them under federal protections.

However, Myron was a lawyer and political operative. He took large sums of cash in return for changing the minds of legislators, facts be damned.

He had achieved prominence by lobbying for brutal dictators throughout the world. His work involved convincing the U.S. Government that these heads of state were worthy of arms deals and financial assistance, no matter how many of their citizens they jailed and how much cash they embezzled. Myron became known as the guy who could burnish the reputation of anyone—even the autocrat who executed his rivals with artillery.

Currently, his clients were an assortment of commercial

interests, including developers who wanted to raze protected manatee habitat and boat manufacturers who wanted to end the go-slow manatee speed zones. Together, they formed a super PAC that claimed its purpose was improving the lives of manatees. Myron called it the "Sea Cow Amelioration Movement," or SCAM.

He had done everything right with SCAM. He took congressmen on the Commerce Committee out to lunch and slipped unobtrusive envelopes fat with 500-dollar-bills under their surf and turf plates. He got them highly coveted tickets to University of Florida and Florida State games. In one regrettable incident, he hired strippers for a state senator who had a heart attack after being smeared with peanut butter. And that was just the beginning of his efforts.

Those were the traditional, Old-Boys'-Network tactics. He prided himself, however, in being a master of the New School of persuasion. He knew traditional and digital marketing better than any of his competitors. So why weren't his clients satisfied by his impressive results?

His favorite campaign was the one we've all seen endlessly on TV during Prime Time. It was the infamous "Boats Don't Kill Manatees; Manatees Kill Manatees" campaign. The ad copy explained that suicidal manatees were to blame for the explosion in the manatee death rate due to boat-manatee collisions. Manatees hated America, the ads explained, and they were willing to do anything to cripple our economy, to harm the boating industry, cause job losses, and destroy families. The manatee terrorists weren't just hurting working people, they were killing an American way of life: the God-given right to motor at full speed through the waterways, beer in hand, your girlfriend sunbathing on the bow in a bikini, your mullet hairstyle flapping in the wind.

His second-favorite campaign was, "Sea Cows Are What's for Dinner." The ads asked, why don't we eat sea cows like we eat land cows? It went further by saying every manatee you kill with your boat could feed a dozen starving families. It was Bob Pistaulover's idea, and he thought this strategy was brilliant.

But the problem was that it was illegal to harvest manatees. And, according to descendants of the early Florida pioneers, manatee meat wasn't very good unless you were an Eskimo accustomed to eating walruses. The market also, apparently, didn't think it was a good idea. Nor did the Fish and Wildlife Service, which walloped him with huge fines.

Pistaulover was not happy. He was the largest contributor of cash from the alliance of boat manufacturers and boating accessory companies that had hired him. Bob was tired of all his efforts to persuade the public and public officials to take away the manatees' protected status and end the manatee speed zones. Bob's solution, at least in his eyes, was much simpler.

He wanted to kill all the manatees. Any way possible.

If there weren't any more manatees, they wouldn't need to be protected. And boaters could have the time of their lives, encouraging more people to become boaters themselves, buying more boats and boat stuff.

Myron had to admit it was a good strategy, despite its utter immorality. After all, his job had nothing to do with morality.

But Bob Pistaulover had no patience for lobbying and advertising.

Myron tried to explain to him that environmental regulations were easy to reverse if you had the right state legislature or U.S. Congress. It just took a while. You needed a bit of patience.

Pistaulover didn't have patience for that, either. He was about to introduce a new line of boats that were all about speed.

They weren't built for the ocean where you could go as fast as you wanted. They needed protected inland estuaries and rivers. The habitat that held manatees. No one could go full bore with one of Pistaulover's new boats if he had to slow down to idle speed for manatee zones.

Manatee zones had to be eliminated. And the best way to do so, in Pistaulover's view, was to eliminate all manatees.

Was he also okay with eliminating people who found out about their plan? Because that's where this was heading. Myron would not tell his client this, of course, to give him plausible deniability if things went sideways. Hopefully, Manny wouldn't let that happen.

For a brief instant, Myron wondered if he was okay with murder. But he quickly shrugged the question away. All he cared about were results. As long as he wasn't tied to any murders, he was okay with them.

Does that mean he shouldn't meet the prisoner? No, he wanted to interrogate the man himself. He didn't trust Manny's competence with this. Manny supplied muscle, not intelligence.

14

HUNTING LESSONS

Contrary to popular belief, vampires do dream. Dreams of their former human lives seem like black and white compared to the vivid colors of their vampire existence. If they were vampires for decades or centuries, their storehouse of vampire dreams far exceeded those based on memories of their pitifully short human lives.

But Maria, only recently turned, dreamed of her childhood, of being held by her human mother, who stroked her hair and caressed her cheek.

She awoke in a dark room on a wide, musty bed, the tiniest crack of daylight showing on the bottom of the window shade. Someone was caressing her face.

It was Sylvia, entwined with her beneath the sheets.

"When darkness falls, I want you to teach me to hunt," Maria said.

"Why hunt when your prey is delivered fresh to your door?"

"I must stop drinking the druggy blood," Maria said. "I've told you a hundred times. I've relapsed and I hate myself for it."

"The drugs shouldn't affect you," Sylvia said. "It's your imagination."

"I know what it's like to be high, and I don't want it anymore. Anyway, I need to learn to hunt humans. Every vampire should know how to do that. You can't depend on always having drugs to lure prey here."

"True."

"Your maker taught you to hunt, no?"

"He did. I suppose I must play the role of your maker now. It's an enormous responsibility. It means you must be true to me until the end of time."

Maria felt Sylvia's eyes staring at her face in the darkness.

What Maria truly wanted was her mother, who had died when Maria was just fourteen. Her stepfather abused her after that, forcing her to run away and survive on the streets until addiction got her in its clutches.

"Yes, I'll be true to you if you truly do what's best for me," Maria said.

"All right, then. Come nightfall, we'll go on a little hunting expedition."

"First, we will begin with easier prey," Sylvia said. "Fortunately, we have many of them here in Florida."

They stood just beyond a pool of light at the end of a parking lot. They were outside the Chinese all-you-can-eat buffet. The place was crowded with senior citizens.

"Many of them eat so early that they're out of here and home before sunset," Sylvia said. "But this time of year, when the sun sets early, you'll have more prey to choose from. We'll let you select your victim. I want to assess your judgement."

"I need to know how to mesmerize them first, don't I?"

"We'll get to that. Right now, choose the oldest, feeblest one you can find. You'll easily be able to overcome them, and their memory might be hazy enough to forget the details about you."

Maria watched diners leave the restaurant in groups large and small. Finally, she spotted a little old man inching across the parking lot with a walker. His car sat near the dumpster.

"I'm going to ask him if he needs any help," Maria said.

"Are you certain?"

"Yeah. I won't find anyone easier than him."

"Okay, then. Take him behind the dumpster and bite him right here." Sylvia traced her finger on her own jugular vein. "Just a quick bite, a quick drink. Then run away as fast as you can."

Maria nodded and tried to build up courage. She reminded herself that she had drunk from the newspaper delivery man outside the witch's home. This prey should be even easier, she thought as she walked toward the man and soon caught up with him.

"Good evening sir, how was your meal?"

He didn't answer. He wore large hearing aids protruding behind each ear.

She got in front of him. "Sir, can I help you get in your car?"

She worried that he'd be frightened, but he looked at her with a knowing grin.

"Thank you but no, young lady," he said. "I'm quite all right."

They were near his car now, in the dumpster's shadow. She had to strike. It was now or never.

She grabbed him by the arms and yanked him toward the dumpster. But she couldn't move him. He stood immobile, like an iron statue.

Then he hissed at her like a cat. He opened his mouth, baring sharp fangs.

And threw her across the parking lot. She landed on a BMW, setting off the car alarm.

A hand grabbed her by the back of her blouse and pulled her away from the car into the shadows beneath a clump of areca palms. She looked up expecting to see Sylvia, but it was the old man.

"Are you inexperienced or just stupid?" he asked.

"I guess I'm both."

"I could tell immediately, you're a vampire," he said. "You should have recognized me as one."

"I didn't think—"

"You didn't think an eighty-year-old man would be a vampire? You're wrong. This is Florida. It's full of geriatric vampires like me. Most of us were turned by lazy vampires like you who hunt old people because it's easier."

"I'm learning how to hunt. My maker was destroyed before she could teach me," Maria said. "But wait a minute, why are you, a vampire, going to a restaurant?"

"So I can dine on the diners. At these buffets they're so immersed in loading their plates with as much food as they can fit, it's easy to get a quick bite of them behind the General Tso's Chicken and nobody notices. Come here on a night when they have snow crab legs. You won't believe how easy it is."

"Thank you, sir."

"You're welcome. Now be more careful whom you attack."

Maria returned to Sylvia, who was laughing.

"You saw what happened?"

"All of it. Try again, but not with a vampire."

"How was I supposed to know he was a vampire? That's another thing I need to learn."

"You knew he was a vampire. Just as I did. You weren't listening to your senses, though. Don't think only of how you'll attack. Your senses are so heightened compared to when you were a human. Open them up, read your prey. Allow your prey to tell you how you should attack."

Maria nodded, even though she didn't fully understand what Sylvia meant.

"Now try again. And don't mess up, or we'll have to move to another location."

Maria was frustrated, but her hunger forced her to circle the parking lot until she saw another solitary diner leaving the restaurant. It was a man again, but younger than the first, probably in his late-sixties. He had a toothpick protruding from his mouth and wore a baseball cap, a skinny fellow with a potbelly. He strolled to his car with a newspaper under his arm.

"Excuse me, sir," Maria said, emerging from the shadows. "I hate to ask, but could you give me a ride to the nearest supermarket? My car is in the shop."

She put on her most seductive airs, cocking her hips just so.

He took the bait.

"Sure, I'll give you a ride. At least you're not asking me for money."

Looking at her with unhidden lust, he opened the passenger door of his Oldsmobile for her. She slid into the seat, giving him a view of her cleavage. He got into the driver's seat and leered at her.

"There's a Super Cheaper a few miles away," he said. "How's that?"

"Perfect," she said. "I'm so grateful for your help."

"It's too dangerous for a pretty young thing like you to be walking around at night by yourself." He shifted to reverse and looked in the rearview mirror.

"What's a handsome man like you doing by yourself?" she asked in a voice that sounded comically sultry.

But he didn't think it was comical. He shifted back to park and stared at her with a grin like he couldn't believe his luck.

So she leaned toward him as if for a kiss. He leaned toward her.

And she sank her fangs into his neck, finding the jugular perfectly. Hot, delicious blood poured into her mouth and her hunger pangs ceased.

She quickly disengaged. He stared at her, stunned.

"I'll see you here tomorrow night and we'll do even more," she whispered, her lips close to his ears.

His old-man hairy ears.

She slipped out of the car and returned to Sylvia.

"Ah, success this time, I see," Sylvia said.

"I used seduction, since I don't know mesmerization."

"It's almost the same thing."

"I want to learn, though. I'd rather hunt younger prey. A handsome guy next time would be nice."

"Remember, prey is prey," Sylvia said. "Don't allow sexual attraction to become involved. It messes with your judgement. All you should focus on is what prey is available, vulnerable, and opportune."

"I understand. But there is someone I want to attack, and she is not vulnerable at all."

"And who would this person be?"

"The witch whose magic destroyed my maker," Maria said. "I tried to kill her once before, and I couldn't. I want to drain her to the point of death and then turn her."

"You? You're too inexperienced to be a maker. You couldn't teach her anything."

"I don't want to teach her. I want to torment her until the

end of time."

"That's not how it works in the vampire world," Sylvia said with a weary smile. "Ah, you have so much to learn."

The vampires returned to Enrico's home. They could have driven, but Sylvia insisted they travel by foot. She showed Maria how vampires who were young in body age could move multiple times faster than a human, so fast, in fact, they could do it undetected by the human eye. Plus, their endurance was unimaginable to a human. The seven-mile walk took less than ten minutes, and Maria didn't feel the least bit tired.

"I feel fantastic!" Maria said. "The animal blood I drank didn't make me feel this good."

"What animals did you feed upon?"

"Raccoons, possums, rodents. A dog, once," Maria said, feeling vaguely ashamed.

"Blood gives us more than nutrients. We also get a boost from the creature's life force. Larger creatures and more advanced species have more life force. Humans are the most advanced, and since we came from humans, their blood is the best of all."

"How long does this feeling last?"

"After you've fed, your energy is at its peak," Sylvia said. "If you ever have to fight or do something that requires great strength, that's the time to do it. By the time dawn arrives, you'll feel normal again."

"The night is still young. How about teaching me mesmerizing?"

"I was planning on feeding on one of our house guests and then binge-watching Downton Abbey."

"Being a vampire sounds like a summer vacation that never ends. Who pays for the electricity and your streaming services?"

"That's a good question and one I'll answer because you're obviously destitute and need to hear this. Some vampires, when turned, have the assets they accumulated when human. If they invest it properly, they'll have hundreds of years to compound interest. That's the case with Enrico. He was in finance and was loaded when he was turned, so he had no problem living off his wealth. There are some good vampire financial managers who can help manage your portfolio, not that you'll need to hire one.

"Some vampires have to keep their jobs," she continued, "which is okay if they work the night shift or if they're office workers working remotely. Being a vampire causes a lot of complications once you outlive the normal human lifespan, you know, dealing with Social Security and all that. I'll explain at another time. Some vampires make a living from crime in all the same ways humans do it. And the rest of us vampires, we become part of a hive and basically freeload off the leader. In my case, it's Enrico. He was also my maker, back in 1901, so I feel totally at home here."

"Am I part of your hive now?" Maria asked.

"You're my guest," Sylvia said, putting an arm around her. "If Enrico wants you, you can join. You must swear fealty to him, and there's a ritual to perform. It's kind of like a wedding, except with blood, fire, and agony. Even more agony than wedding planning."

Maria wondered if this was an option she'd like. It sure beat being homeless and living in someone's shed. But she wasn't sure she wanted to be Sylvia's plaything for eternity.

"So, if Enrico wanted me in his hive, would I be allowed to bring Lucy, my vampire cave bear?"

"Enrico prefers human pets, but he might allow Lucy to stay in the detached garage where we bury our victims."

"That would be really kind of him."

"Now, are you done with all your questions? Lord and Lady Grantham await me on video."

"Don't forget the mesmerizing."

Sylvia sighed. "One lesson tonight. More at another time. Follow me."

She walked at a normal pace along the sidewalk toward the commercial street. Maria went beside her. Any passerby would see only a younger woman and a slightly older one, perhaps friends or coworkers, headed for a watering hole.

Would they have any inkling we're vampires? Maria wondered.

"Mesmerizing prey is similar to hypnosis," Sylvia said. "But you're not helping them quit smoking or lose weight. You're not getting them to do embarrassing acts on stage. You're getting them to do two things: submit to you completely and then have amnesia about the entire attack."

"Hypnosis sounds corny."

"You won't think so when your fangs are buried in your prey's neck. Now, you've probably seen hypnotists use various methods to induce the hypnotic state. This isn't like that. The vampire's power of mesmerizing is partly psychological, and partly supernatural. It begins with your eyes. You must make eye contact with your prey."

"Okay."

"Intense eye contact. You must put yourself in a semi trance-like state, too."

Sylvia stopped and gripped Maria by each shoulder.

"Watch my eyes," she said. "I'm focusing my mind one hundred percent on you: on your breathing, your heart beating. I'm imagining your blood flowing through your blood vessels. I can hear it flowing. Now, do you see my eyes?"

"Your pupils are dilating big-time."

"Right. That's when they feel themselves drawn into your inner being. That's when the supernatural is kicking in, binding them to your will much more powerfully than hypnosis could. You'll feel it when they're under your power. Then, all you have to do is give them commands, whether it's simply to remain still or to follow you somewhere. When you're done feeding, you command them to forget you and everything you did while holding their gaze again. Then you wave your hand like so."

Sylvia waved her flattened hand, palm out, across Maria's face, breaking the hold of her eyes.

"Then you walk away. I would have put you under, but vampires can't mesmerize other vampires."

"My maker could," Maria said. "She could also turn into a bat."

"Well, you're talking about a whole different species of vampire. Modern-human vampires can't. Ready to give it a try?"

"Um, I don't know."

"Let's find a stranger and do it. Not to feed on them. I want you to put them under briefly and then wake them up. You need to build confidence before you use it for feeding."

"Hey, I used my seductive charms tonight, and they worked just as well."

"Best not to limit your diet to horny old men who lack common sense. There's no shortage of them in the world, but you'll need more options than that."

"So I go up to someone and just catch their eyes?"

"Yeah, but try not to come across as a weirdo. Often you have to speak to them first. Look over there. See those people waiting for a table? Try it on one of them?"

"Right in public?"

"Yes. But don't bite anyone."

Maria crossed the street to the sidewalk in front of a restaurant with a large outdoor seating area and a line of people snaking out the door from the hostess station. A group of friends chatted with each other. Behind them was a woman staring out into space. A perfect target.

"Excuse me," Maria said. "Is the food here good enough to be worth the wait?"

Maria tried to catch her eyes, but a man in line next to the woman was talking on his phone. Loudly.

"You tell him the offer isn't good enough," the man said. "We need more money up front."

Maria tried to ignore him. But he went on and on, posing as a big-shot dealmaker. The woman, possibly his date, kept rolling her eyes in annoyance. Maria couldn't lock them with hers.

She wanted to roll her eyes, too. The man was such a loud buffoon.

She turned her attention to him and caught his eyes. They looked at her questioningly.

She put herself into the trance-like state and imagined the inner workings of his circulatory system. His eyes couldn't leave hers.

Suddenly, the man stopped talking. He gazed into her eyes with his mouth open.

"Hello, Mac?" said a voice over the phone. "You still there?"

"Throw your phone across the street," Maria commanded him.

He threw his phone. it sailed across the parallel-parked cars and the slow-moving traffic. It landed on a group of men standing outside a bar.

The diners sitting outside of the restaurant broke into applause. Maria gave a little bow, then waved her hand across the face of the loudmouth. He became cogent again and stared at the hand that had held his phone, wondering where it had gone.

Just in time to see the burly man, whose head the phone had hit, come running across the street to teach him a lesson.

"Nice job," Sylvia said when Maria returned to her. "There might be hope for you yet."

MEANWHILE, just a short vampire-sprint away in distance, but a million miles away in trendiness, there was another line of diners waiting to be served. They were elderly vampires queued up after the Blood Bus pulled into the parking lot, awaiting pint bags of fresh whole blood.

Agnes listened to the conversation behind her.

"Henry was at the all-you-can-eat buffet tonight and—you won't believe this—a vampire tried to attack him?"

"Oh, no!"

"It was a young woman, some punk covered with tattoos and piercings. She didn't even realize Henry is a vampire! Clearly, she had no idea about how to hunt."

"Did she not have a maker to teach her?"

"I guess not."

Agnes had s strong suspicion it was the young vampire she had seen stoned on drug-laden blood in the house on Stork Street. The poor young thing needed some benevolent vampires to take her in and protect her.

Such as a kindly vampire step-grandparent. There were plenty of candidates here at Squid Tower.

Well, perhaps not so many kindly ones.

15

MAGICK KINGDOM

Matt lay on the concrete floor of a rental storage facility. The tiny room was empty except for him, a bucket, and a bottle of water they had generously tossed at his head after they pushed him in here hours ago. The only light came from the crack at the bottom of the door.

His head still throbbed from whatever they had thumped him with. His wrists and ankles burned from the overly tight zip ties that had bound him until they cut the one from his ankles when they walked him here from the truck. His wallet and cellphone had been taken.

He was depressed, to say the least.

Missy and he had made good progress in uncovering the plot to poison manatees. Too good, in fact, because he got close enough to the perpetrators to end up in here. But he didn't have any inkling of a motive.

Why would anyone want to kill adorable manatees in the first place? Well, adorable except for Seymour. Why was it such a vast enterprise, dumping the potion all over the state? And why were they willing to kidnap him and risk serious jail time for this?

He had told his abductors he was a reporter, to justify why he was snooping. That turned out to have been a bad idea, the moron who said that realized as he lay in the dark with his hands bound.

This plot was as if the perpetrators wanted to eradicate manatees from the state. But why? What was the profit in that? What was the pleasure in that, unless you simply hated animals and the environment?

Or unless you hated environmental regulations concerning the endangered creatures.

And who would suffer from such regulations? Developers. People who hated to cruise slowly in the manatee zones.

But how would making the manatees even more endangered help their cause? It wouldn't; it would only lead to more regulations.

If they helped increase the population of manatees, some restrictions would probably be eased. But not all of them. They would have to eliminate *all* manatees to make *all* the restrictions go away.

Could that be their goal? It was bonkers. And, yeah, it was evil, as if that ever stopped anyone from being bonkers.

Matt lay there for hours trying to make sense of this scheme. It was his best way to avoid thinking too much about what was going to happen to him.

A key rattled in the padlock outside the door. It snapped open, and the door swung open. He squinted in the artificial light from the hallway. There weren't any windows, so he didn't know if it was day or night.

Three men were silhouetted by the light. One was short and shaped like a bowling ball with legs.

An overhead light came on. The men weren't the same ones who put him here. The short, fat one was bald and past middle age. He wore a white goatee. Beside him was a tall and muscular man, with a bushy brown beard and eyes too close together. Hanging back behind them was a guy in a black blazer with sunglasses and slicked-back hair.

The men stood just outside the doorway, appraising him. Then they came inside and closed the door.

"Why is a reporter interested in me?" the little guy asked. He had a slight Spanish accent, Cuban or Puerto Rican.

"I was just taking a leak at the park," Matt said. "I didn't even notice your guys."

"They said they also saw you at the boat ramp near Stuart. Do you take leaks at every boat ramp along the east coast of Florida?"

"You know what happens to your prostate when you get older."

The big guy leaned down and slapped Matt's face. Matt had to suppress the urge to kick him back.

"There's been a lot of dumping of substances in waters lately," Matt said. "Why is that?"

"What are you, some tree hugger?"

"Ever hear of the Clean Waters Act?"

"Since you're so interested, all we're dumping is beer. Pumpkin-spice beer. We're doing the world a favor. And the beer won't hurt anything."

"Except manatees," Matt said.

The man's eyes squinted. Matt realized he'd said too much.

"I'm sure that's a coincidence," the little man said.

The man in the black blazer spoke for the first time. "Are you a flack for Mothers for Manatees?"

"No. I know very little about them."

"Have you written any articles about this dumping?"

It was time to lie.

"I have. They haven't been published yet, but my editor has them. If anything should happen to me, she would know why and in what direction to point the authorities."

The little old guy laughed.

"That depends on what should happen to you. You might have a tragic accident that wouldn't seem suspicious at all."

Matt realized he couldn't talk his way out of this.

"Why do you have a problem with manatees?" Matt asked.

"I don't care one way or another about them," the little man said. "I'm just doing my job, which is to dump the beer and end the pumpkin-beer madness."

"But it's killing them."

"Beer can't kill anyone."

"It killed my uncle Bobby," the big guy said. "He drank an entire case of beer and a half a bottle of moonshine."

"Shut up," the little guy said. "A fifty-gallon barrel of beer won't do any damage in a large body of water."

"There's something in the liquid that's killing them."

"Pumpkin-pie spices? Cinnamon and nutmeg is killing them?"

"And ginger and allspice," the big guy said.

"I told you to shut up."

"C'mon, you know it's not really beer," Matt said.

"All I know is what they tell me," the little guy said.

"Who tells you? Who do you guys work for?"

"People punks like you could never touch."

143

"I've heard all I need," the guy in the blazer said. "I was never here. Wait until I've left the property before you do anything."

He walked away, his expensive shoes slapping along the hallway.

The little old guy turned to his goon. "Tell Ricky to get over here and help you take care of this tree hugger. I think he'll accidentally fall into Ricky's wood-chipper. Wouldn't that be ironic?"

The big guy smiled, though it was doubtful he knew what ironic meant. They turned off the light and left the room. The padlock clicked.

Missy's LOCATOR spell and its orb of energy always amazed her with its power. The problem was, it showed Missy an image of where Matt was, but it didn't give her an address or GPS coordinates. Ancient earth magick didn't work that way.

She could make the orb rise above the location, basically like zooming out on a satellite map to give her an idea of what part of town he was in, but she then had to cross reference the image with an actual satellite map and find a match. She also brought it down to the front of the location, so she saw that it was a commercial storage facility, but she couldn't move the orb down the street to find a street sign. The orb was bound to Matt's energy almost magnetically. It took hours in front of her computer before she determined the facility was south of the airport.

It was interesting that this spell, which existed since the Medieval times or earlier, depended on modern technology. But back in the old days, the subject you were searching for probably wasn't too far away, and you were more likely to recognize the surroundings in the vision the orb sent you.

When she finally got on the road to Orlando, she had no plan of how to rescue Matt. Nevertheless, she brought the Red Dragon talisman to increase the power of her magick. And she brought Seymour. She didn't enjoy his eyes roving over her as she drove for two and half hours, but she figured his Ranger training would be useful.

"What if they move him before we get there?" Seymour asked.

"I'll need to cast the spell again to find where he went."

"We might not have time. If they move him, it might be to dispose of him."

Missy looked at him with alarm. She knew Matt was in danger, but she hadn't imagined they would kill him. All of this was her fault for getting him involved.

Her grip on the steering wheel tightened, and she increased their speed as she wove through the traffic on Florida's Turnpike.

"Maybe we should discuss a plan of attack," Missy said.

"Do you know the exact storage unit he's in?"

"No, the spell is not that precise. I'm going to use something other than magick: Call his name and follow his voice if he answers."

"If there are no guards around, that should work. If there are, I'll take them out. Then you use your magick to unlock the unit and we bring him to the car and get the heck out of there. They'll assume no one knows where he is, so we'll have the element of surprise on our side."

"I wish you were armed," Missy said. "I'm sure the bad guys are."

"I don't need a gun. And remember what I said about killing."

"Right."

They drove in silence. Until they saw signs for a service plaza ahead.

"I'm hungry," Seymour said.

"How could you be hungry? I'm too terrified to be hungry."

"Manatees graze constantly all day long. Maybe it's a coping mechanism."

"They only have fast-food joints at these service plazas."

"I'm sure I can find a salad."

"We're on a rescue mission. We're kind of in a hurry."

"I'll be quick. I promise."

She sighed and took the left-hand exit into the service plaza. She handed Seymour some cash like he was her kid and waited in the car.

Seymour emerged from the building with his bag of food, wearing a hat with Micky Mouse ears.

"You've got to be kidding."

"They have a souvenir counter."

"I know, but why are you being a goofball? We're about to go into danger."

"When I was a kid, I always wanted to go to Disney World. I guess being in human form brings out these strange urges."

"We're not going to Disney World," she said as they merged back onto the Turnpike.

"We'll be in the neighborhood. I figured after we rescue Matt, we could have a little fun."

She shook her head in exasperation.

"C'mon, please?" he begged.

She ignored him for the rest of the way to Orlando.

When they reached their exit, she checked the mapping app

on her phone and navigated to an avenue lined with seedy strip malls and auto repair shops. A few blocks later, she recognized the storage center. She found a parking spot in front, close to an exit. It was a three-story storage facility where you accessed the units from inside the building. That made an escape more complicated.

Missy took a deep breath and said, "Let's go."

They got out of the car. As they walked to the entrance, Missy glanced at Seymour.

"Take those stupid ears off!"

"Why?"

"This is serious. Lives are on the line."

"If the bad guys are here, they'll think I'm a tourist and pay no attention to me."

"You're so annoying. Should we split up to cover the building faster?"

"No. We need to cover each other. Let's start at the third floor and work our way down."

They took the elevator up. It opened at the end of the floor, which had two parallel hallways running the length of the building. Missy peered down each hallway. They were empty. Going down the left hallway past the numbered steel doors with padlocks, she called Matt's name loudly enough, she hoped, to be heard from behind a closed door, but not so loud someone on another floor would hear her.

Matt didn't answer. They walked down the other hallway. Again, her calls went unanswered.

"What if he's unconscious?" Seymour asked.

"If we strike out on all the floors, I'll try a different spell and see if I detect his presence in the building. If I don't, we can assume he was taken somewhere else."

To be killed, she thought. Because of me.

"I'm hoping we get lucky," Seymour said.

"I don't believe in luck. All sorts of crazy supernatural things are a daily reality for me, but not luck."

The elevator was still waiting on their floor and they rode it to the second floor. The door opened.

And three men waited outside. One of them was Matt. The two other men stood on either side of him, each holding an arm. A windbreaker was draped over his wrists in an unsuccessful attempt to hide that they were bound.

Matt's eyes doubled in size at the sight of Missy, but he said nothing. Dried blood caked his hair.

"Going down?" Missy asked.

The largest man, bearded and taller than Matt, grunted. He wasn't happy to see people in the elevator. He and the other guy, a Hispanic with a tattoo on his cheek, pushed Matt ahead of them onto the elevator. Missy moved aside and pressed the button for the first floor, but she stayed near the door.

Seymour was right about his Mickey Mouse ears making him look innocuous. The two thugs ignored him and stared ahead at the door, Seymour standing behind them.

They only had one floor to travel. Was Seymour going to attack?

A snapping sound was her answer.

The big guy with the beard went down onto one knee and screamed. His partner twirled to face Seymour and was met with an open-palm punch that broke his nose, followed by a rabbit punch to his throat. He gurgled and dropped to the floor.

The elevator door opened at the ground floor.

"Get out of here now!" Seymour shouted. Missy yanked Matt out of the elevator while Seymour held the bearded guy in a choke hold.

"You've always had impeccable timing," Matt said. "I was on my way to be fed into a woodchipper."

The icy grip on her heart returned.

"Are you serious, or is that Matt sarcasm?"

"I'm serious," he said. "They hate people as much as they hate manatees, I guess. I think they're trying to wipe out all of the manatees."

"Yep, that's what they're doing."

They jumped in the car and Missy started the engine, moving the car just before the exit lane to the street.

"Hurry up, Seymour," she said. "There was no time to cast any spells on those thugs, so Seymour is on his own."

"He seemed to have things under control."

Just then Seymour sprinted from the building and hopped in the back seat. He still wore his Mickey Mouse ears, though they were now crooked and one of the ears was bent.

Missy floored it and raced from the parking lot—as much as a four-cylinder with 100,000 miles can race. Soon, they were on the Turnpike headed south.

"I was hoping we would go to Disney World," Seymour said.

"Enough," Missy said.

"Do you think they saw your car?" Matt asked. "It wouldn't be hard for them to catch us on the Turnpike, especially with so few exits."

"Don't worry," Seymour said. "They were too preoccupied when I left them to see what her car looks like. Or to even get off the elevator."

"Good," Matt said. "And I didn't notice anyone else around to spot us."

"We know one of their crew is in jail right now," Missy said.

She caught Matt up about the visitor to her home after Matt went missing.

"So these guys work for a lawyer?" he asked.

"Yep. We don't know who, though."

"That means there's big money involved," Matt said. "Can you believe their cover story is they're dumping unwanted pumpkin-spice ale?"

"I can believe someone would dump that nasty stuff," Missy said. "And it explains the large amounts of nutmeg in Seymour's system."

"Well, you're a wine drinker. You wouldn't appreciate a pumpkin ale. Anyway, maybe the brewery really was producing beer, but with black magic in it. It's a good cover story."

"Do you think they'll continue to use the brewery?" Missy asked.

"Why not? Even though we know what's really going on, no one would believe us. Especially if they're really making beer. There's nothing toxic in it except the black magic."

"I happen to believe that cinnamon and nutmeg in beer are toxins," Missy said.

"Hey, do you know anything about the Mothers for Manatees?" Matt asked. "They wanted to know if I worked with them."

"The thug that broke into my house asked about them, too," Missy said. "I emailed their organization, along with others, to alert them that someone was harming manatees. I didn't know they were so feared."

"We should team up with them," Seymour said. "We could use some additional muscle."

16

GRANNY RAIDERS

A few decades ago when home brewing became a fad, Lenny tried it. And failed miserably. Bottles of his nearly flat, bitter concoction with sediment on the bottom gathered dust in his garage because none of his friends or family wanted to drink it. Neither did he.

And here he was, brew master of a craft brewery. Well, that's what the other guys called him as a joke. His actual job was pizza chef at a takeout place, supplemented by income from odd jobs for Manny. The jobs truly were odd. Sometimes, his task was delivering boxes. Sometimes, providing security at a political event. A bunch of times, it was beating up guys, usually sniveling losers in expensive suits. Often, it was bringing bags of money to politicians.

Today, it was pretending to be a brew master and super-vising three guys who knew what they were doing: making thousands of gallons of a beverage that wasn't really beer and tasted even worse than Lenny's failed home brews.

"Hey, Lenny!" Tony called from the brew room. "We're low on cinnamon and allspice."

"Gotcha. I'll order some more. It'll be here tomorrow."

The "beer" they were pretending to make had many of the ingredients of pumpkin-spice ale, Lenny's favorite. But why were they adding toadstools? That sounded disgusting.

Another odd thing about this operation was putting the beer not into kegs but into fifty-gallon plastic barrels. Lenny had overheard the guys mentioning that the "beer" they were making was promptly dumped out afterwards in various bodies of water around the state. In fact, trucks returned empty barrels to the brewery every day. At first, Lenny carefully washed the barrels before they were filled again until everyone laughed at him and said the cleaning wasn't necessary.

The oddest thing about this job was the person he reported to. It wasn't Manny directly; it was a kooky old lady named Ruth Bent. The "beer" they were making was according to her recipe. She yelled at Lenny if the mixture wasn't perfect.

Since the "beer" didn't need fermentation, the crew completed a batch every night. That was when the old lady showed up, always with a cigarette in her mouth and a bunch of scratch-off lottery tickets in her hand.

"Win anything tonight, Mrs. Bent?" Lenny asked with a welcoming smile.

"Buzz off, moron. Even when I win, I never seem to break even. It sucks trying to get by when you're old. Even Medicare drains me dry with Part B and D and all these premiums I can't make sense of."

"Doesn't Manny pay you a fair wage?"

"Manny doesn't pay me. I was hired by Manny's boss. He hired Manny to help me make my potion. None of you morons would be here if it wasn't for me."

"Oh. Well, thank you, I guess."

"Don't thank me until I make sure you didn't screw up my potion."

She half-walked, half-limped to the main holding tank. It was stainless steel with brass fittings. The entire brewery had much nicer equipment than this nasty "beer" potion deserved. Mrs. Bent opened a spigot at the bottom of the tank and a trickle of liquid filled a pint glass adorned with the brewery's logo.

She held it up to the light, tilting it back and forth as if she were a connoisseur judging a rare brew.

Then she smelled it, taking deep breaths with her nose stuck deep into the glass. Finally, she took a small sip which made Lenny cringe every time he saw her do that.

"Not bad," she said. "A little heavy on the nutmeg, but that's just as well. Okay, it's time for you boys to get your butts out of here while I do my thing."

No one knew what her "thing" was, though T.J. claimed she was performing a Santeria ritual while Pete swore that it was voodoo. All Lenny knew was that she demanded absolute privacy, so everyone had to clear out of the building and kill time in the parking lot until she told them it was all right for them to return indoors. Then they would fill the barrels and load them onto trucks. They were short a guy because Frank hadn't shown up for work. Word was that he'd been arrested.

Lenny had noticed that the air in the brew room always smelled of burning candles snuffed out. So maybe she really was doing some religious ritual. Weren't there monks in Europe who make beer? He bet they blessed each batch. Maybe this was the same kind of thing.

So out into the parking lot they went. Tony and T.J. sat on the loading dock platform vaping. Pete paced back and forth, talking really fast on his phone. And Lenny just stared off into space, thinking about his girlfriend.

Then all hell broke loose.

Headlights flooded the mostly empty parking lot as four cars poured in. They screeched to a halt, facing the building, bathing it with their lights. Lenny blinked stupidly, blinded.

Was this a police raid? But they had done nothing wrong. Unless drugs were secretly pumped into their potion. Or was this a gang demanding tribute? Or maybe it had something to do with Mrs. Bent's weird religious stuff.

Actually, it was a bunch of really pissed off old ladies running towards the building with axes and baseball bats in hand.

Lenny didn't want to get his head cracked, so he didn't move while the ladies rushed into the front door of the brewery.

A woman and two men exited the fourth car. They weren't as old as the attacking grannies. The larger of the two men looked at Lenny and the guys with menace in his eyes, but he didn't stop to hassle them.

Clanging and crashing came from inside. Lenny and the guys exchanged glances.

"I guess we better go in there. We have to protect this operation or Manny will kill us." And he knew Manny might do just that, literally.

By the time the crew returned inside, it was already too late.

WHEN MISSY MET with the local chapter of Mothers for Manatees the day before, she held nothing back. Except the black magic part, of course. She explained the substance created by the bad guys harmed only manatees and that it was being dumped all across the state to eradicate manatees and somehow boost the profits of powerful entities she hadn't identified yet.

She was pleased to learn that Mothers for Manatees had already mobilized statewide to monitor and guard waterways frequented by manatees. But now that Missy knew the location where the deadly substance was made, the ladies agreed to form a raiding party.

Missy, Matt, and Seymour simply came along for the ride.

Inside the brewery, it was a scene just like a raid by the hatchet-wielding Carrie Nation during Prohibition. Ladies cracked open barrels and tanks with axes amid a flood of spilled liquid. Only here, it was a black-magic potion instead of beer. The ladies smashed everything in sight, even tables and equipment that had nothing to do with the potion.

Missy hadn't realized her mother was here. The fireballs shooting from the back room clued her in.

Missy had been raised by adoptive parents, having been told her parents died when she was an infant. She believed that until midlife when she discovered her mother was not, in fact, dead. Her mother, Ophelia Lawthorne, had given Missy away. And then she went on to live a productive life as a black-magic sorceress, selling her services to the highest bidder under the alias of Ruth Bent.

Now it appeared that the highest bidder was a lawyer working to eliminate manatees from Florida.

"What the heck is that?" asked Tameka, dodging a ball of flame.

"That's some serious black magic," Missy replied. "I suggest you guys wait outside while I handle this."

As the ladies headed for the exit, the four men who worked here tried to get in. When they saw the fireballs, and got bonked by the ladies' baseball bats, they quickly retreated.

Seymour and Matt joined the ladies to force the men to leave the property.

A dark-dyed haired figure appeared in the window of the brewing area. Yes, it was her mother.

"What are you doing here?" Missy demanded.

"What does it look like I'm doing—I'm enchanting a potion. What are you doing here?"

"I'm going to stop you."

"Why are you always meddling with my magic?" her mother asked petulantly.

"What do you mean 'always'? I got you to undo your magic on one occasion. And you tried to kill me in the process."

"Just because you're my daughter doesn't mean you have to act like I'm a monster."

"You *are* a monster. You practice black magic. You summon demons and kill people."

"Don't get all holier-than-thou with me."

"Most monsters I know are holier than you. You're evil. It says so on your business card."

"No, it doesn't. I have a new one now. I'm going to ask you to leave. I have work to finish."

"I'm afraid I can't leave," Missy said, keeping alert for a sudden attack. "I can't allow you to kill any more manatees."

"I'm not killing anything. I'm just making a potion."

"Don't play dumb with me. A client paid you to make this potion, which they're using to wipe out innocent animals."

"You wouldn't be complaining if it was bedbugs or cockroaches."

"What you're doing isn't just immoral, it's illegal," Missy said. "I could have you arrested."

"You know they can't prove my potion kills them. The potion is just a delivery mechanism for the magic, and as far as science is concerned, magic doesn't exist. So go ahead, call the cops. You and your Greenie friends will be the ones arrested."

Ophelia pulled a battered pack of cigarettes from her jeans and lit one with a defiant expression.

Missy didn't know what to do. How could she stop her mother short of killing her?

She couldn't physically harm this old woman standing in front of her, whether she was her mother or not. If she needed to do so to save her own life, that was a different story. But the anger and resentment inside wasn't great enough for Missy to knock her down and strangle her. Nor could Missy take her prisoner. Her mother was right; the police wouldn't arrest her. Instead, they'd charge the Mothers for Manatees for property destruction.

"Your niece, my cousin Darla, told me you killed my father," Missy said in a low, calm voice.

"Nonsense."

"You summoned a demon to do it."

"Why would I do that?"

"You tell me. Because he was more powerful than you and achieved that through benevolent earth magick, so you were jealous of him?"

Her mother cackled. "Jealous? Pretty little earth magick spells are nothing to be jealous about. He couldn't even kill anything with his magick."

"Right. That's the point. Why would he want to kill anything?"

"That's what power is all about. Power over other people, other creatures. Making them bend to your will. Killing them if you want them out of your way."

"That's abuse of power," Missy said. "Power is for healing, protecting, creating."

Her mother laughed again, but broke into serious coughing.

"I believe you did kill my father," Missy said.

"A demon killed him. I saw it happen."

"You were there?"

"Your father was loading the dishwasher when a really powerful demon, I believe it was Belphegor, appeared out of the detergent compartment and tore him to pieces. It was very traumatic."

"Yeah, it must have been a horrible way to go."

"I mean, it was traumatic for me."

What a narcissist, Missy thought.

"Then you shouldn't have summoned the demon."

"I told you I didn't."

"The more I talk with you, the more I believe you summoned it. Remember, you tried to kill me when I went to your house."

"You were there for hostile purposes. I was only defending myself and testing how powerful your magick is."

The door opened and Matt came into the pub area.

"I heard on my scanner that the police are on their way here," he said. "We should go."

Her mother smiled victoriously.

"This isn't the last you'll hear from me," Missy said to her. "If the manatees don't stop dying, I'm coming after you. And I just might put aside my morals and seriously hurt you. Or worse."

"The manatees will stop dying when there are none left to die. And I have a faster, better way to do it than this potion."

Her mother smiled defiantly at her. Then went into a coughing fit.

Missy wanted to smack her mother around, but not to kill her. She wanted to get her mother charged in her father's death, even if it took her years to find the evidence that would incriminate her.

"I didn't stop her," she said to Matt and Seymour before getting in the car. "I can't stop her from doing evil stuff if she wants. The only way would be to kill her. And I couldn't bring myself to do that."

"I understand," said Seymour. "Lubblubb died because of the sorceress. But I wouldn't be able to kill her either."

MYRON HAD DEPENDED upon Manny for too many years and they'd both grown sloppy. Myron should have had other fixers lined up, but it was all too easy to call Manny. And Manny was screwing up. His men allowed the reporter to escape. He allowed the crazy manatee ladies to discover the brewery and raid the place, destroying the equipment.

But it was too late to use someone new, too risky to share information with anyone else. So he ordered Manny to find a new location in which to manufacture the potion. He located a shuttered dairy in a rural area of Central Florida that was willing to accept a tenant and was far from prying eyes.

He called Ruth Bent to tell her about the new location. He promised Manny would find her an acceptable motel within an easy drive of the dairy.

"Are you going to take care of those people, so they don't raid us again?" she asked.

"The Mothers for Manatees? We can't kill them."

"Why not?"

"No one messes with the Mothers for Manatees. There are too many of them. And they're too vicious. That would start a war that would put me out of business."

"And there's that nurse and her two male companions."

"Sure, we could kill them."

Myron didn't mention that Manny had already blown opportunities to take out two of them.

"I don't know about this, Myron." The click of a cigarette lighter came over the phone. "This incremental strategy of yours leaves us too exposed to discovery. I say we go big. Get this done fast."

"How?"

"I have more magic up my sleeve. I can go very ugly and very evil."

"I thought we were already very evil."

"You haven't seen anything yet," she said as she broke into a coughing fit.

17

ROCK-STAR HAIR

M others for Manatees sent Missy photos of the boat they had attacked. Missy studied them and had a strange idea. She called up Matt.

"Can you find out what the registration number was on the boat where the F-W-C officer was murdered?" she asked.

"It was a fake number," Matt replied.

"I know, but I'm looking at pictures the Mothers for Manatees took of the boat they attacked last night. I know it's a stretch, but what if this was the same boat?"

"That would be incredible," Matt said. "Let me make some calls to the F-W-C and the police and see if I can pry that out of them."

A half out later, he called back.

"Got it," he said. "FL 3712 WZ."

"Oh, my. It *is* the same boat!"

"I assume it fled the scene after it was damaged?"

"Yeah. The Mothers for Manatees were too busy messing up the land-based crew to chase after them. They said they didn't have a way to restrain them until the law arrived, even if they had caught them."

"Let's assume the boat is being repaired," Matt said. "We should visit all the boat-repair shops in the area and see if we're lucky enough to find it."

"Make a list and I'll come pick you up."

It turned out there were a lot of businesses that repaired boats. Even narrowing them down to those that repaired fiber-glass hulls resulted in seven businesses within a reasonable drive. Some owners were more cooperative than others. None had seen the boat in the photos.

"This is so tedious," Missy said after the second day of canvassing. "And we can't even be sure the boat is being repaired in our area. Or repaired at all."

"I'm sure a boat that expensive will get repaired. And yes, being a reporter can mean a lot of wasted time. If you don't get a specific lead from someone, you just have to be methodical and rule out possibilities."

"And you like your job?"

"I used to."

Missy stopped in front of the bungalow where Matt lived to drop him off.

"What do we do now?" she asked.

"Remember the boat manufacturer that owned the boat busted for dumping?"

"Of course. Where I trespassed to detect if any magic was there."

"Right. Shouldn't we check them out, too? Maybe this was one of their boats again. They could repair it themselves. But I don't know how we could search the place without getting caught."

"I might have a way," Missy said. "With magick."

"Every reporter needs a friend who's a witch."

MISSY DROVE to the Barbarian Boat Works plant to orient her sense of direction and refresh her memory of the route. She didn't turn into the entrance, though. She parked at the side of the road far from the gate and stared at the property for a while before driving home.

When she prepped for the spell casting, she added a contemporary accessory to this ancient spell that had first been written in a grimoire over a thousand years ago. It was her laptop computer. She pulled up a satellite view of the boat factory to keep it fresh in her mind.

Seymour was out doing Lord knows what, so she had the house to herself. After shutting the cats in her bedroom, she drew a magick circle on her kitchen floor, lit five candles, and cleared her mind.

Very few witches had the power of astral travel. To truly achieve it with intentionality required more than meditation or a spell; it required the natural paranormal abilities Missy was born with, of which her telekinesis was one. But she couldn't astral travel at will and to a specific destination without casting the powerful and ancient spell.

She gathered the energies within her and then those from the five elements: earth, water, fire, spirit, and air. The element of air was especially important. She had opened all the windows of the house and inhaled deeply the breeze that came inside from the east winds over the Atlantic. It had a hint of brine scent even here, two miles from the beach.

She recited the Latin words of the spell, which were written in a series of verses. The power charm she held in her left hand throbbed with energy as if it were electrified. A tingling engulfed her hand and traveled up her arm to her heart. It rose to her head, and it felt as if her hair was standing on end.

Then the tingling reached her mind. Her vision went white. And she had the sensation of being unmoored like a hot-air balloon with its ropes untied.

She felt as if she were rising from the tile floor until she hovered by the ceiling. She looked down and her body was still kneeling on the floor.

Her soul had been untethered from her body. Her mind was still connected to it, and that was how she saw the world.

She flew to her destination, not like a bird traveling over the countryside, but like a bullet arriving in only seconds.

She hovered high above the boat works. Her view of the scene was not from her memory. She saw it in crisp detail. In fact, she could see better than with her eyes. It was as if she perceived the essence of the place, the truth of the people who worked there and the history of the structures, their materials, the winds and rains they had withstood over the years.

She swooped down to a lower elevation. Now her flying was like a bird's, gliding gracefully, circling when she wanted to.

She made several passes above the buildings. A forklift moved a finished boat outside of the main assembly building. A pair of men walked from the building to a smaller one.

She descended farther. She passed through walls as if they didn't exist and flew slowly across the factory floor, where the boats were framed out, where the fiberglass was poured and cured, past the painting stations, where the electrical wiring was installed, where the seats and accessories were added.

She nearly touched the heads of the workers, and none of them showed any signs of sensing she was there.

There were no older boats in here, so she searched the

smaller outbuildings. They mostly contained supplies and materials. One was a garage that serviced the forklifts and other vehicles.

Then she saw what appeared to be a repair shop and parked outside it was a large boat on a trailer covered with a tarp. She hovered just above it.

She couldn't physically remove the tarp, but, with enough concentration, she could see through it.

One side of the hull had scrapes and cracks. Dark scuff marks crossed it horizontally. And there on the bow was the registration number: FL 3712 WZ.

This was the boat the Mothers for Manatees had attacked. The very same vessel used by the murderers of the FWC officer.

A tall man exited the building. He had a huge mane of blond hair like a 1980s rocker. He lit a cigarette and stared at the nearby river. Then his eyes darted upward at Missy.

There's no way he can see me, she told herself. I'm just a spiritual presence; I'm invisible. He must have felt the unusual energy concentrated above him like a disturbance in the air pressure. People don't need extrasensory perception to sense the presence of magick. There is plenty of it in the world, and most people are blind to it as they plod through their mundane lives.

But this man did sense it, even if he didn't understand it.

And in him, Missy detected malice. And evil. She had no rational reason for feeling that way, but in her heart, she knew she was right.

She had a feeling he was on this boat the night the officer was killed: the tall blond man the witness mentioned.

Since Missy was present here in the boatyard as merely a psychic manifestation, she didn't have her full array of spells at her disposal. But she could probe this man, just as she had searched the buildings for the boat.

She focused on the malice he radiated. She zoomed into his thoughts, where darkness dwelled. Random images appeared to her. A petite, dark-haired woman that he loved. A young child, his son. A Brooklyn street. A sign above a butcher shop with the Cyrillic letters of Russian words. A smoky back room where men talked crudely and drank vodka. A heavy, bald man gesturing with a bottle in his hand, barking orders.

The blond man with a handgun in his hand on a snowy day. She recoiled at his memory of shooting a man wearing a fur hat in the back of the head. It was a memory he savored. There were other killings, too. He enjoyed remembering them like a man tallying his prized possessions.

She probed more deeply, making the man twitch uncomfortably, though he didn't know why. An arrest by undercover cops. Interrogations in a windowless room. Signing documents.

Then a memory that made him most uncomfortable: He was on the witness stand answering questions while the heavy bald man sat at a table next to attorneys, glaring at him with death in his eyes.

After that, the memories became pleasant again. Swimming in the surf on a Florida beach. Fishing with his young son from a small boat in a lake. Racing along the Intracoastal in a powerful boat.

Then another prized memory: pointing his gun at the forehead of a man in a uniform, silhouetted by a spotlight. Anger at the officer for coming onto his boat. Pulling the trigger twice and seeing the shocked expression on the officer's bloody face as he fell overboard, disappearing beneath the water.

There was the briefest moment of guilt, angry at himself for losing his self-control. But it was overcome by his satisfaction from the fast, brutal act that rid him and his crew of the nuisance.

This man was the killer of the FWC officer. Missy felt tainted by witnessing the event, almost as if she had been there, guilty by association.

The blond man was becoming agitated. She had probed his mind for too long. She had to leave at once.

Missy turned her attention to images of her house. And willed herself to be there.

Almost instantly, she was floating above her metal roof.

The gutter on the west side is clogged, she thought. I hate getting on the ladder to clean the banyan leaves from the gutters.

And as the mundane matters of the world began to distract her mind, she passed through the roof and into her kitchen, settling back into her body that had been waiting for her on the floor.

She opened her eyes, wiped away part of the magick circle, and ended the spell.

She felt exhausted. Although the magick had empowered her, the mind and soul had done all the hard work. But she had important things to do.

"I found the boat," she said to Matt as soon as he answered the phone. "It's at Barbarian Boat Works. They haven't even repaired it yet."

"That's awesome!" he said.

"And I saw a man there, a tall guy with blond hair, whom I'm certain was the one the witness saw when the F-W-C officer was murdered."

"Now we need to get an appointment to speak with the company's owner before we notify the police about the boat. He won't speak with anyone after that. And how do you know the man you saw was on the boat that night?"

"Do you really need to ask?"

"Ah, I see. Impressive work, Ms. Witch."

Seymour walked into the kitchen and waved to her before grabbing a head of lettuce from the fridge.

"I was just telling Matt that I located the boat the Mothers for Manatees damaged. It was at Barbarian Boat Works," she said to Seymour, putting her phone on speaker. "And I found the man who shot the F-W-C officer."

"The company's president, Bob Pistaulover, is very active politically," Matt said over the speaker. "I can see him hiring the lawyer who is running this plot."

"We need to kidnap him so Missy can use her truth spell," Seymour said.

Matt snickered. "Seriously? We should commit a major felony on a rich, well-connected guy?"

"Yeah," Seymour said. "And allow me to add an extra felony by beating the crap out of the murderous scumbag. Same with the thug who works for him."

"Not a good idea. They say manatees don't do well in prison."

"You're just too scared to do it."

"Children, stop bickering," Missy said. "We don't need to kidnap and beat anyone. I only need to get in a room with him."

"And then beat him," Seymour said.

"There goes the conventional wisdom that manatees are gentle creatures," Matt said.

"The aggression comes from my human side. Which was what I thought I left behind."

"If we could figure out a way to get a meeting with him or be in a social situation, I could cast the truth spell on him,"

Missy said. "Let me ask my contacts at Mothers for Manatees. They have some very wealthy benefactors who might have a connection with him."

"Wouldn't that organization and Pistaulover be sworn enemies?" Matt asked.

"The rich are in a world of their own where their wealth transcends any differences in politics. If you keep your donations secret, that is. Let me see what I can arrange."

"What about the shooter?" Seymour asked. "What are you going to do about him?"

Matt said, "Missy identified him with her magick."

"Magick isn't exactly admissible in a court of law," Missy explained. "We'll have to find another way to point the police in his direction."

"After we kick his butt," Seymour said.

"How now, sea cow?" Matt said before Missy disconnected the call.

18

UNDEAD TRESPASSING

M aria slipped quietly from bed before daylight had
fully bled from the sky.

"What are you doing?" Sylvia murmured.

Maria inwardly cursed. Sylvia never woke up this early. It
was like she watched her every move lately.

"I can't sleep. I'm going to take a brief walk."

"Night hasn't completely fallen. You can't walk now."

"It will be dark by the time I'm dressed."

"Come back to bed, little one."

"I want to go out and hunt."

"So confident of your new skills already?" Sylvia asked. "We
have two college kids passed out in the living room to feed us.
Let's stay in tonight and watch movies."

"If you weren't on a blood diet, I'd say you're going to get fat.
You never want to do anything but stay in bed."

Sylvia looked hurt.

"I'm sorry, Sylvia. I'm very grateful for you. But I still have a
score to settle."

"Are you talking about that witch who destroyed your maker?"

"Yes."

"You must have truly loved your maker."

"No, not really, although she was kind to me when I was held captive by their clan. Mostly, I'm angry for all that's happened to me in my loser life. My mother died and left me. My stepfather betrayed me. I lived on the streets as an addict, and then I finally got a chance to get clean. I followed all the rules in rehab and was ready to start a new life. But then, I got sold to vampires to be their dairy cow.

"I didn't want to be a vampire," Maria went on. "I didn't buy all the promises and talk of how great it was to have heightened senses and supernatural powers and being immortal. I just wanted to lead the normal, human life I never had. And then look what happens: My maker is killed, and I end up homeless, on the street again, not even knowing how to feed myself."

Sylvia sat in bed, hugging her knees, listening with a pained expression.

"So, yeah, I'm angry," Maria said. "And, yeah, I want to take my anger out on someone. That person is the witch. The one who put me out on the street again."

"You have a home now," Sylvia said.

"Sort of. I'm a good little plaything for you until I get Enrico to like me."

Sylvia frowned. "He won't like you if you do something stupid. You can't turn the witch into a vampire just to make her suffer. That's against the Vampire Code. It's a perversion of the powers of vampirism."

"I didn't know there was a Vampire Code."

"You will find out when you are staked to death for violating it. There is a lot you still don't know. That is why you shouldn't be foolish."

"Can I kill the witch if I don't make her a vampire?"

"Of course you can kill her. And you can make her a vampire, but you would then have to take on the responsibilities of being her maker. And, I'm sorry, but you don't know enough to teach her anything."

"Okay. I understand. So, can I go kill her now? I promise I'll be back soon, and we can watch movies."

"Yes. But no witnesses. And pick me up some batteries for my remote on your way home."

MARIA HAD BEEN STALKING the witch Missy Mindle for quite some time. She knew where she worked, and after the failed attempt at the witch's house, this time Maria would try to catch her unaware at her workplace.

The witch went to places where old people lived. At first, Maria thought the witch worked as a cleaning lady, visiting clients in two condo communities on the beach and sometimes in town. Once, she sneaked into one of the buildings and listened with her heightened hearing at the door of a condo the witch had entered. Based on the conversation and the pumping of a blood pressure cuff, Maria deduced that the witch was giving a medical exam. On another visit, she helped a patient with complaints about his digestion. When she heard the elderly patient complain about back pain from sleeping in his coffin, she realized something surprising.

The patients were vampires. And in the complex of two buildings next door, her eavesdropping taught her that the patients here were elderly werewolves. Even in a fifty-five-plus retirement building at the foot of the Intracoastal Waterway bridge, where the witch came for a daytime appointment and the residents walking around were definitely human, the patient the witch was visiting spoke about the health complaints unique to elderly trolls.

Maria hadn't known that supernatural creatures existed besides vampires. And they had a human home health nurse? Maria thought it was crazy.

She wondered if killing the nurse would be a bad thing. She would be denying these elderly monsters the healthcare they needed and obviously had a hard time finding if they had to resort to a human nurse.

But her brief moment of conscience faded. Yes, she would still kill the witch. Let the old fogeys find a new nurse.

Tonight, Maria stalked the grounds of Squid Tower on the beach where the vampires lived. She found the witch's beat-up car in the parking lot. It was time to devise a plan.

Attacking the witch in the building was too risky. There might be security cameras and a neighbor could come along during the attack. It would be best to ambush her outside.

Maria decided to wait at the witch's car and intercept her when she was leaving at the end of her shift. Hopefully, that would be before sunrise, but late enough that the vampire residents wouldn't be wandering around.

Unlike the failed attempt at her home, the witch would be more surprised and wouldn't have a house to retreat into. Maria would use her new ability of mesmerizing to subdue the witch quickly and then drain her to death.

Maria crawled beneath the car and prepared for a long wait. There would be no movies with Sylvia tonight.

She was near the pickleball courts where the old vampires played with more enthusiasm than seemed appropriate. Tennis shoes squeaked and scraped on the court; racquets slammed balls with ping pong-like clopping sounds. Players cheered and cursed. Some guy shouted that if he could kill the Earl of Gloucester with a battle-ax, he could sure as heck ace his next serve.

And then something awkward happened. A ball left the court and landed in the parking lot nearby. It bounced ever closer until it rolled under the witch's car and came to rest against Maria's face.

She immediately tossed it out into the open.

But then the upside-down face of an old man appeared under the car. He stared at her. He was a vampire.

"Are you okay under there? Did someone run you over? Some folks here are pretty bad drivers."

"I'm fine, thanks," Maria said. "I'm just resting."

"Why are you resting under a car?"

"The asphalt is still warm from the day's sun. I like the warmth. I'm like a snake that way."

"Are you homeless, young lady?"

"No," Maria said. "I'm here visiting my grandmother."

"Awww, that's nice. Who is she? Maybe I know her."

"Um, her name is Grandma."

The vampire's upside-down face frowned.

"Grandma Annie."

"I don't know any Annie. Well, I hope the asphalt stays warm for you. Thanks for tossing the ball out from there."

That was too close for comfort. She knew the old vampire would tell his friends there was a weird woman under the car. She would have to find a new ambush spot.

AGNES' phone rang. It was from the gatehouse.

"Yo, Mrs. Geberich. It's Bernie at the gate."

"Yes, Bernie."

"I got this feeling we have a trespasser on the property. It's a vampire, but definitely not one of us. And they didn't come in through the gate, so it's not a visitor."

"Thank you, Bernie. Can you leave your station for a few moments and take a quick walk around the property?"

"Will do, Mrs. G."

Everyone knew that Bernie was not the sharpest pencil in the box. That's why he didn't quit his job when he was a human working the night shift at a condo tower filled with vampires. Once he was turned, it didn't make him any smarter, but he did gain the extra sensory benefits of being a vampire. One of which is being able to sense the presence of other vampires.

Agnes was concerned about the trespasser. Ever since the community had survived the hostile takeover by a clan of Neanderthal vampires that had kidnapped some residents, she hadn't gotten over the trauma.

Soon, Bernie called again.

"I didn't see anyone, Mrs. G. But I had to walk around fast because I couldn't leave the gate unmanned—I mean, un-vampired—for long."

She thanked him and called one of the board members, Bill. He was a gun enthusiast who had militaristic fantasies. Naturally, he was happy to accept her request to scout the community.

"Your guns are not required," Agnes said. "Remember, it's a vampire, so bring a spear instead."

"I always go on patrol with a full array of weaponry," said Bill, who had never served in the military despite his swagger. "I'll contact you via satellite phone with intel."

"Bill, just use your cellphone. You're not even leaving the property."

"Roger that," he said before clicking off.

This was how the vampires had to deal with crime in their community. It was always a bad idea to allow the Jellyfish Beach Police Department on the property. At least one member of the force knew about vampires and wouldn't hesitate to stake someone any chance he got.

Agnes waited to hear back from Bill for nearly forty minutes. He was taking much more time than a sane vampire needed. She worried he was in trouble.

Until she surveyed the grounds from her balcony and saw him. He was wearing camouflage and low-crawling commando-style across the grass in front of the building, dragging himself forward with his elbows while holding a semi-automatic rifle.

Why do our vampires keep reelecting this guy to the board? she wondered.

MISSY WRAPPED up her final patient visit of the evening. Edna Spleene in 742 had called with severe gastric distress. It turned out that Edna had been a chocolate addict her entire adult human life, and even now in her undead state couldn't quell the cravings.

Everyone knows you should never give chocolate to dogs. Why don't they know that you never give it to vampires, either? Or any human food, for that matter. Edna knew better, but couldn't resist. Maybe after a few hundred more years of being a vampire, she'll get over the chocolate addiction.

Missy had a proprietary potion that vampires could

consume that would relieve their stomach distress. Made with various herbs and a bit of her magick, it was more effective than any over-the-counter digestive remedy that humans used.

Missy took the elevator and crossed the lobby. It was a couple of hours before dawn, and she was exhausted.

She opened the lobby door and instantly wished she hadn't.

The vampire who had attacked her at home was blocking her path. The tattooed young woman stood just beyond the protection zone of Missy's amulet.

"Don't tell me you've come to apologize," Missy said.

"Oh, yes, I'm so sorry for my embarrassing behavior before."

The vampire was trying to catch her eyes, trying to mesmerize her.

Missy looked away. "I forgive you. If you'll just let me get to my car."

"No, I mean, I'm really sorry. Don't I look sorry?"

Missy refused to look at her face. She stared at the vampire's body instead. It was coiled, ready to spring at her.

"Please stop trying to mesmerize me," Missy said in a calm voice. "Let me get into my car."

The vampire moved toward her, then recoiled from the anti-vampire amulet. In the previous attack, she had overcome the mild magick, so Missy was already casting a protection spell.

"Put your hands in the air or this spear will go right through your heart," said a soldier decked out in tactical gear who had crept up behind the vampire. It was Bill. Only a vampire could move so silently that another vampire wouldn't hear him. You'd think she would have, though, with all the guns and body armor he was wearing.

The young woman turned to face him and hissed.

"Listen here," Bill said, "we don't allow any hunting or

blood-letting in our community. And technically, you're trespassing. Leave Missy alone and go home."

"I have unfinished business with the witch," the young vampire said. "She killed my maker."

"Oh, your maker was one of those Neanderthal vampires who terrorized our community? Who kidnapped me and held me captive as a hostage? Why, I ought to stake you right now."

He prodded her with the sharp end of the wooden spear and forced her against the wall of the building. The spear remained touching her abdomen, angled for a quick stab upwards beneath her ribcage to her heart.

Missy moved away from the door and farther from the vampire, while she called Agnes and told her what was going on.

"Don't stake her, Bill," Missy said. "Or at least wait until Agnes gets down here."

When Agnes arrived, she didn't behave the way Missy expected.

At only four-foot-eleven and barely a hundred pounds, Agnes carried a serious weight of authority. Her presence alone was enough to instill calm and respect. She walked straight to the younger vampire without any concern or defensive moves. She touched the woman's arm. Bill tensed, preparing to thrust his spear.

"Sweetness, it's going to be okay," Agnes said to the vampire. "You've been through a lot of trauma, and I want you to know you have a home with us if you need a place to stay."

"What?" Bill exclaimed. "Her maker was one of the Neanderthals."

"I remember how difficult it was adjusting when I began my new life as a vampire. Though, as you can see, I was a lot older than you." Agnes chuckled. "My maker left me not long afterwards."

"Really?"

"I tried to track her down over the years, only to find out she'd been killed by human peasants. So, I had to learn about vampire life mostly on my own."

The young vampire seemed to relax a bit.

"I lost my maker, too," she said. "Because of this witch."

"Missy is an honorary member of our vampire community. She's helped us in so many ways. I'm sorry to say that your maker was part of a clan that was evil."

"It was." A bright red bloody tear rolled down the young vampire's face. "I don't know what to do. I'm so angry and confused."

"That's perfectly normal," Agnes said. "Why don't you come inside and have a pint of fresh blood. And we can talk. You'll be safe with me."

The young vampire nodded and followed Agnes inside and down the hall to the community rooms.

Missy was astounded. Bill appeared to be as well. And a little disappointed.

"I was so close to staking her," he said. "Is Agnes crazy to invite her inside?"

"Maybe you should go in there and check on them. But, I need to get out of here before I get the young punk riled up again."

Missy drove home, hoping that Agnes' sweet grandmotherly side would tame the feral vampire.

ODD COUPLES

aria sat quietly while Agnes microwaved two bags of whole blood. Agnes wanted to make the young vampire as comfortable as possible, so she would listen with an open mind to advice from a 1,500-year-old.

"O positive," Agnes said. "Intense flavor with hints of copper."

"Drinking out of a bag is gross," Maria said.

"You'd rather put your mouth on a vermin-covered animal?"

"I've moved up to humans now,"

"Drug addicts. You shouldn't be feeding on them. I saw you the other night in the living room of that house, high as a kite."

Maria hung her head in shame. "Yeah."

The microwave dinged. Agnes removed the bags and inserted sippy straws. She handed a bag to Maria.

"Here you are. Nice, clean sustenance."

The young woman took a reluctant sip and pleasure lit up her face. She continued drinking hungrily.

"Now tell me," Agnes said, "are you happy living in that house?"

"I guess. It's better than living on the streets. Sylvia has been very nice to me and is teaching me stuff like my maker would have done. But she can be kind of possessive."

"Have you been invited into their hive?"

"No. Not yet."

"I have to say, those vampires are a dubious bunch."

"Why were you in their home?" Maria asked.

"I'm leading an outreach campaign to the vampires in Jellyfish Beach. I'm not sure if you're aware of this, but the leader of your maker's clan wanted to rule all the vampires in a hostile takeover."

"I was their prisoner," Maria said.

"Around here, we vampires like our independence. We want to enjoy our deathstyle in the lovely Florida nights for eternity. We don't want to serve a master. So, I'm setting up an informal network among the vampires here for providing assistance to each other if needed. Because someone like you shouldn't be forced to choose between homelessness and living in an unhealthy house."

Maria nodded. "I don't want to be around drugs."

"If drugs bring the police to that house, it would be a disaster. Vampires don't do well in jail. Or, worse, the police could stake you on the spot."

"Really?"

"Yes," Agnes said. "The few police officers who know about vampires perform extrajudicial executions. One member of that hive captured an undercover officer and wanted to feed on him. When the officer was released, I had to mesmerize him to make him forget about the house, but he could return. And this is not only about one hive. If they discover any vampire, it will endanger all the vampires in Jellyfish Beach and the entire region."

"Okay, I get it," Maria said sullenly.

Agnes realized she was lecturing too much.

"You can stay here if you wish," she said. "I live alone in a three-bedroom."

"Sylvia would be upset if I don't return tonight. She'll come looking for me."

"You're free to do as you choose. For now. If you join their hive, you must obey Enrico."

Maria only nodded.

"Did you know your grandmothers when you were a child?" Agnes asked.

"I remember my abuela. She died shortly after my mom died. My abuela was such a good cook. And she sang songs to me."

Agnes smiled. "I loved all my grandchildren. I outlived them, of course. They had children and their children had children, and so on, but I couldn't be part of the family anymore once I was turned. I know that somewhere in the world, there are people who descended from me. I wonder, sometimes, who they are."

Maria had finished her bag of blood and seemed relaxed at last.

"I should be going," she said. "Thank you for not harming me after I tried to attack your witch."

"I understand how you feel. But don't try to attack her ever again. You don't owe your maker anything, and soon you will be rid of any attachment you feel for her."

"Maybe."

Maria smiled at her and then disappeared into the night.

Agnes was surprised at herself for offering Maria a place to stay. She felt like the mother figure for all of Squid Tower and didn't need on her hands a young, inexperienced vampire with problems.

But, to be honest, having someone young around would be a nice change of pace from a homeowners association of undead curmudgeons who complained as frequently as they breathed.

WHEN SHE FOUND her toilet seat left up, Missy had had enough. Why was Seymour using her bathroom? He was creepy enough with his constant stares at her cleavage. Invading the master bath was beyond the pale.

She was tired of the footprints of canal water on her hardwood floors, the clumps of hydrilla on the kitchen floor and clogging up the guest bathroom tub. The endless bags of potato chips he went through (why a mer-manatee would like chips, she had no idea).

He should have been able to shift back into a manatee by now.

"How have you been feeling?" she asked him while she sipped tea in the kitchen, and he munched on a head of romaine.

"I'm still grieving for Lubblubb. But I'll never get over that loss."

"I'm sorry. But I was referring to your health since you were poisoned by the potion."

"Oh. I'm feeling much better, thanks. As you can see," he patted his bulging belly, "I've gained back most of my weight."

"Have you been able to shift to your manatee form?"

"No. I don't understand why I can't. I tried yesterday in the canal. And yes, I know you told me to swim at the municipal pool instead, but I can't transform into a thousand-pound manatee in a public pool, can I?"

"I should think not," Missy said. "I've been wondering if it might be time to try some magick."

"You have a spell to turn me into a manatee?"

"No, but I have spells that cure ailments that only supernatural creatures get. Maybe I can restore your natural ability to shift."

He chewed thoughtfully on the lettuce. "It's worth a try."

"Are you ready now?"

"Now? 'Seinfeld' reruns are on TV soon."

"It's dark out so neighbors won't see."

"Well, okay. I guess it's worth a shot. But don't get your hopes up."

Missy retrieved the grimoire that had the spell instructions. It was *The Book of Saint Cyprian*, printed in the sixteen hundreds. It had been owned by Don Mateo, when he was alive, and the blank pages at the end of the book were filled densely with text scrawled in ink by the wizard when he had lived with the Timucuan people after he came to Florida. The spells included many taught to him by the shaman of the native American tribe. Some of these were for healing supernatural ills. As far as she knew, this handwritten addendum was the only existing written record of these spells.

She kept the grimoire in the bottom of a cat litter box, under the liner, sealed in double plastic food storage bags. The litter box was the one place thieves would never look.

She took photos with her phone of a few spells she believed might work and placed the grimoire back in hiding. On her workbench in the garage were vials and baggies containing the herbs, powders, feathers, and other ingredients the spells called for. She packed these in a tote bag and called for Seymour to meet her in the car.

Rather than trespass in her neighbor's yard to reach the canal, Missy drove a few blocks away to vacant land beside a bridge over the canal. She parked on the grass and they climbed down the bank to the water.

"Privacy, please," Seymour said.

"No problem, believe me," Missy replied, turning her back to him as he disrobed.

After he waded into the water, she set to work on the spell she believed most likely to work.

Don Mateo's notes had said this was a spell to restore the ability of shamans to see the future, for the harvest to be plentiful, and to cure foot fungus. But it also mentioned that it helped shamans shift into coyotes.

Coyotes, manatees. Why not?

She had also brought along the Red Dragon talisman to give her additional power for the spells, since they were not her own.

After she gathered her internal energies, she drew upon those of the five elements, particularly water, as she stood next to the canal. Coastal Florida had immense energies within the network of freshwater canals, lakes, and the water table underground. There was also the nearby Intracoastal Waterway and ocean, the saltwater being particularly charged with energy.

"Kneel in the water next to the shore," she told Seymour.

He complied. Turning her head to avoid seeing anything she didn't want to see, she sprinkled rare Florida herbs and mineral powders over his body. Then she laid a long osprey feather atop his shoulders. As she recited the Timucuan words to the spell which Don Mateo had written phonetically, she cupped canal water in one hand and sprinkled it upon Seymour's head.

She took hold of the Red Dragon and read the final words of the spell while the talisman's power surged in her hand and ran through her body.

"Let your abilities return," she said as the power left her body, and Seymour shuddered when it hit him.

Nothing happened. He was still human. But the spell was only supposed to restore his ability to shift. The rest was up to him.

"Try to shift now," she said.

He waded into deeper water, his flabby buttocks jiggling, and dove in. Floating on his stomach with his face in the water, he looked like a drowning victim.

And then, the strangest sight: His body swelled, as if inflated by air.

Her eyes were not playing tricks on her in the darkness. He really was growing fatter. And taller.

She'd seen werewolves shift from human to wolf, and it was unpleasant to watch. Their transformation looked painful as their joints dislocated, jaws distended, teeth and nails grew. Even the fur sprouting all over their bodies appeared uncomfortable.

But Seymour's transformation was slow, and gentle, just like the creature he was becoming.

In the moonlight, his skin turned gray and when he raised an arm out of the water, it was now a flipper. He gave a slow flip of the giant paddle tail he now had instead of two legs. He dove beneath the surface and when his head emerged, it was the head of a manatee, seal-like snout with whiskers and jowls.

"It worked! Seymour, you did it!"

He rolled around in joy, then dove beneath the surface. A few minutes later, his snout came up for air.

"Now you can return to the wild," she called to him. "You're free now. Goodbye, and live in happiness as your true self."

She waved to him. He slapped the water with his tail as he swam away.

The song "Born Free" played in her mind.

A tear rolled down her cheek. Why was she sad? She should be celebrating that he was finally out of her home.

She sighed, packed her supplies, and picked up Seymour's discarded clothes from the ground. Before she got into her car, she took a last look at the canal.

A fat, naked man was stepping out of it onto the bank, dripping with water.

"Wait, what happened?" she asked. "Why did you shift back to human?"

"I told you: 'Seinfeld' is on now."

"Don't you want to go back to your life as a manatee?"

"Of course I do. But not now. We still have work to do in stopping the manatee killers. Lubblubb has to be avenged."

"Well, I think—"

"Face it, Missy, as annoying as I may be, you need my help. You and Matt can't fight these people on your own. And who knows, my Ranger training might come in handy again."

She realized he was right. Any help he provided could be important in this fight.

"Okay. You're right. Get in the car."

"Did you buy me some more potato chips?"

"One bag. That's it. I didn't think I would need more."

BLACK HEART

yron's conference room was the setting for many an amoral and immoral decision. For him, business and politics were all about the bottom line and not the least bit about good intentions and selfless acts. He also provided public relations services to serve as pretty window dressing hiding ugly acts. But he never kidded himself about how far he would stoop to make a buck, and how evil you needed to be to make two bucks.

It was strange, yet fitting, that a sorceress was now in his conference room conjuring up black magic to wipe out the entire population of an endangered species. Was it really so different from lobbying government to gut regulations that would result in the deaths of thousands of people over the years? No, it wasn't. Here he had a woman in a matching sweat suit with a palm tree motif instead of a guy in an expensive Italian suit, but the result was the same.

Okay, granted, the cloud of sulfur here was different. And

the eerie rumbling in the walls. Ruth's plan to summon a demon was making him very nervous.

Ruth knelt atop the polished oak conference table within an inverted pentagram surrounded by a circle drawn with chalk. Large black candles burned at each of the five points of the pentagram, dripping wax on the expensive table. A brass bowl of incense burned in front of her, obscuring her face with a cloud of noxious smoke that resembled burning rubber and gasoline.

The sulfur stench didn't come from the incense bowl. It came from all around the room. It troubled Myron, because he knew the sort of evil entity the odor was associated with. The fallen angel. The Big Guy. The baddest dude of all. Satan. The entity Myron most wanted as a future client.

Ruth chanted ceaselessly while rocking back and forth in a kneeling position. What she uttered sounded like Latin mixed with ancient Greek, with a smattering of Middle Eastern languages that involved a lot of throat clearing.

Her chanting had a hypnotic effect. Myron felt like he was in a trance and floating in an alternate reality. Images flitted across his vision like a movie projected on the walls of the conference room. The movie was basically the story of everything bad in the world, edited together in a dizzying montage of evil. There were scenes of the petty cruelty of a child slapping another child, to a crowd chanting racist words, to a jet dropping bombs on a hospital, to the deliberate burning of a rainforest with small mammals fleeing, their coats on fire. He saw all varieties of humans killing one another throughout history, while others suffered starvation in forced famines at home and in prison camps. He saw the most brutal fascist and communist dictators grinning with glee and Mongols on horseback slaughtering villages, prisoners marching to the killing fields, and morgues filled with terrorism victims.

It was depressing, even for Myron.

The sorceress pulled a dagger from her overstuffed purse, held it aloft and turned it so the blade glittered with the yellow light of the candles. Then she drew it across her left palm.

The drops of blood fell into the bowl of burning incense, and the flames flared up.

Now, the images flickering upon the walls were of Hell itself. No devils with pitchforks, but amorphous blobs that turned out to be faces contorted in agony. Quick images flashed of a half-human, half-goat head with glowing eyes and bone visible through rotting flesh.

Billowing smoke and flames with hints of creatures moving through them. Quick suggestions of unnatural shapes and beasts with five legs, humans with legs where their arms should be. Children with two heads, wolves with human faces, and a man with the head of an octopus.

Ruth's chanting changed to a nasal wail, and Myron snapped out of his waking dream.

"Asmodeus, I summon thee!" she shouted.

Myron hoped the office next door couldn't hear. They were a Christian charity or some sort of do-gooder organization that shouldn't be able to afford the rent in this building. At least she was summoning a demon and not Satan himself.

"Asmodeus, I beg thee to give me the power of Moses to bring a plague upon my enemies. Give me the power on the night of the next full moon, and I shall direct it."

The sulfur stench was overpowering now. Myron fought the urge to gag. The temperature in the room dropped drastically to freezing level. Myron hugged himself as his breath came out in a cloud of vapor.

The table vibrated and rose nearly a foot above the floor. Ruth didn't seem to notice. Her head tilted backwards, her eyes closed, her mouth twisted in rage.

A rumbling like a freight train surrounded the room. It sounded exactly like the Category 4 hurricane that almost destroyed Myron's house last year.

Ruth moaned and cursed in the rumbling bass voice of a large man.

"From first moonrise to final moonset, you shall have the power," she said in the male voice.

The flames in the incense bowl disappeared with an audible "poof." The powders and dried leaves that had burned in it were gone, but there were no ashes. Instead, a black object the size of a softball sat in the bowl.

Myron looked at it more closely. It was a human heart, as black as obsidian and just as hardened.

The floating table lowered and settled down on the floor.

Ruth wiped away a small portion of the chalk circle she was inside and then collapsed on the table. She slept, her chest rising and falling with labored breathing.

Myron didn't know what he was supposed to do, not having attended a demon-summoning before. He was tempted to check on Ruth, but didn't want to mess anything up or piss any demons off.

But when she shifted position and her pink sweatshirt threatened to catch fire from a candle, he moved the candle away from her.

All at once, the candles went out.

Ruth cackled and slowly sat up on the table.

"Oh, that was a doozy," she said. "For a while there, I thought Asmodeus was going to kill me. But the conjuring worked. He gave me the power I need. All I have to do is cast the proper spell during the full moon the day after tomorrow, and the manatees should begin dying at once. By dawn the next day, they'll all be dead."

"What is that thing?" Myron pointed to the black heart on the incense dish.

"It's what it looks like: a black heart. It's the incarnation of the evil in the hearts of humans. Everyone has a little in them, though they mostly suppress it or rise above it. Some people—here's looking at you, Bob Pistaulover—have lots of evil and celebrate it. Or some, such as you and me, humbly make our livings with it. And there it all is, represented by that black stone. That's what will give my spell the power it needs to cause such a massive die-off."

Myron was sorry he asked.

"By the way, I'd like my second payment now," Ruth said. "Deposit it directly in my bank account."

She had demanded an exorbitant bonus on top of her original fee. She said the extensive amount of extra magic she needed to use, and the risk involved justified it. Myron now understood the risk. Demons weren't to be trifled with.

Pistaulover and the others wouldn't object to the additional funding. It sounded like the results they wanted were going to be even greater than they could have dreamed.

MISSY AWOKE from a sound sleep with a sense of dread. It was noon, but the blackout shades kept her bedroom as dark as night. What had awakened her was a blinding light across the back of her eyes.

A major shift in the universe's balance had occurred. An enormous blast of magical energy had been injected into the world, and it was evil energy. Humans wouldn't notice anything different, though many animals would, like they sense the dropping of barometric pressure that signals a coming storm. And witches, at an advanced level like her, would feel it, too.

She went on her computer and at her favorite witches forum were dozens of posts about the shift they had sensed, along with dire threats of what it might mean.

But only Missy knew the real cause. Her mother must have caused it.

The final attack against the manatees had begun.

TRUTH TELLING

Barb McCoy was one of the biggest donors to Mothers
for Manatees. She mostly donated to causes like
historical societies, art museums, and the Save the
Eyebrows Foundation. In short, she picked her charities
according to the lavishness of their annual galas. But she'd
always thought manatees were adorable, and after years of
courting by Mothers for Manatees, she finally opened her
checkbook. Big time.

She convinced Bob Pistaulover to sit down for an interview
with Matt. It would allegedly appear in the CEO's favorite
magazine, *Luxury Power Boats*, or as it was familiarly called,
"Buxom Babes in Bikinis on Big Boats." Barb even convinced
him to do the interview on very short notice the next day.

Matt and Missy arrived in the late afternoon after Missy's
sleep was interrupted by the shift in the universe. It took her a
while to get ready. What do you wear on a day when evil gains
ascendance?

Compared to her astral travel, driving on roads to get to the factory seemed to take forever. It was late enough that many of the workers in the office building had left for the day. A junior sales guy pointed out where the CEO's office was. The door was open. Matt looked inside.

"Sir? I'm Matt Rosen for *Luxury Power Boats Magazine*. Are you ready for us?"

"Yeah, come in," a deep voice said. He didn't sound happy to see them.

Matt entered the office and Missy followed. The enormous creature behind the desk waved them closer.

"Who did you bring with you?" Pistaulover asked.

"This is Missy Mindle, my assistant," Matt replied.

Missy kicked him in his Achille's tendon. He stifled a grunt of pain.

"Let's get this dang thing over with," Pistaulover said. "I'm just doing it as a favor for Barb."

"Don't you want to be on the cover of Big Boats?"

"Only if you do a photo shoot with me and those buxom bikini babes."

"Of course," Matt said with a conspiratorial smile. "Isn't that the point of our publication? Can we sit over there so I have a place to put my voice recorder?"

Matt pointed to a round table surrounded by four chairs. Pistaulover nodded. They waited for him to lift his bulk from his desk chair and plod over to a seat at the table. Missy sat down across from him with her legal pad on which she would pretend to take notes. Matt sat closer to the CEO and turned on his digital voice recorder, setting it on the table near Pistaulover.

The reason Matt requested to do the interview at this table was it provided Missy a way to toss the powder for her truth-telling spell onto Pistaulover's feet under the table without him seeing it. While Matt pitched softball questions to the CEO about his business successes and his philosophies of pleasure boating, Missy recited the words of the spell. While Pistaulover was engrossed in explaining the correlation between an engine's horsepower and a man's virility, Missy reached under the table and tossed the powder. Then she completed the invocation and engaged her energies to activate the spell.

Pistaulover's eyes took on a glassy look. Missy knew the spell was working.

"Are you involved with killing manatees?" she asked abruptly.

"Yes," he answered with a smile. "To the tune of fourteen million dollars."

"But why?" she asked.

"I hate manatees. People think they're cute, but they're actually brutal monsters."

"Manatees? Brutal?"

"I was just a little kid floating on a raft. I had no idea the manatee was there. It came up from beneath me and surfaced, knocking me off the raft. When I tried to get back on it, my bathing suit fell off, and the mean girls laughed at me."

"You're killing manatees because the girls laughed at you?" Matt asked with disbelief.

"No. That's why I hate them. I'm killing them because manatee safety zones are hurting the boat industry. I build boats meant to go fast. What's the sense of buying a fast boat if you have to keep it at idle speed?"

"Oh, my," was all that Missy could manage to say.

"The big, fat slobs are always allowing themselves to get hit by boats. It makes our industry look bad," Pistaulover said, leaning back in his chair, his hands with interlocked fingers resting on his giant belly. "They'll never increase in numbers enough to get removed from the endangered list. So we figured, let's get rid of them altogether. No more worrying about saving them. They're gone, the safety zones are gone, and business goes through the roof. We sell more boats, boaters can go faster, and don't need to worry about hitting manatees or ripping out the sea grass the manatees eat. Developers can build more waterfront homes. Fewer fines when we 'accidentally' spill fuel and battery acid in the water at our factory."

"How are you running this scheme and how big is it? Who all is involved?" Matt asked.

"I have a lawyer who operates in Tallahassee and D.C. He has other clients like me—boat manufacturers, distributors, and retailers. Real estate developers. We've been paying this lawyer big bucks for years to convince legislators to cut regulations, have fewer manatee zones, and downgrade manatees on the endangered lists. But it's a slow, frustrating process. So, I had the brilliant idea of getting rid of the sea cows completely. My lawyer couldn't find a way to do it effectively. He hired hunters to shoot them, but that just inflamed the news media. He tried dumping toxins, but that wasn't effective enough and upset the sport-fishing industry. My lawyer, he's a cunning, evil little guy. . ."

"What's his name?"

"Myron Hickey. As I was saying, he suggested using black magic. Can you believe it, black magic? Turns out he's tried it before on U.S. Congressmen with some success. He's one of those cutthroat, end-justifies-the-means guys. Perfect quality for a lawyer. Anyway, he knows this sorceress for hire. Myron's got a guy who arranges for the sorceress to make large amounts of a magic potion that is harmless to everything but manatees. He finds guys to dump it all around the state where there are populations of the vile monsters."

"Did you help dump this potion?" Missy asked.

"I volunteered a couple of my boats, but it wasn't worth the trouble."

"Did you know the crew of one of your boats killed an F-W-C officer?" Matt asked.

Pistaulover appeared genuinely shocked.

"No," he said. "No one told me that."

"Yeah, he did, while committing crimes for you. And Myron's 'guy' almost killed me," Matt added.

"That Myron. See, I told you he was cutthroat."

It was obvious to Missy that Pistaulover was just as lacking in morals as Myron.

"Where is the sorceress?" she asked.

"I have no idea. She was working out of a brewery here in Jellyfish Beach, but then the Manatee Mafia attacked the brewery and damaged the equipment. Myron set her up somewhere else."

"Where can we find Myron?"

Pistaulover took his wallet from his pocket and removed a business card. He handed it to Missy.

"That's his office. His personal number is written on the back."

The CEO was showing signs of impatience. Even the truth spell couldn't change someone who was impulsive with a short attention span.

"Aren't we going to talk about me some more?" he asked.

"Sure," Missy said. "Do you feel any remorse for killing several hundred manatees?"

"Nope. I regret not doing it faster."

Missy couldn't fathom a man like this.

"Do you cheat on your taxes?" Matt asked.

"All the time. I'll be happy to give you pointers on my

favorite techniques. But I'd rather talk more about my brilliance in business."

"Actually, I think I've got plenty of material on that," Matt said.

"Did you get the quote that I'm a prophet on the future course of boat building?"

"Absolutely. That will be the lead of the story. Thank you for your time."

Missy and Matt left the building as quickly as possible before Pistaulover realized how much he'd said and that it had all been recorded.

"Are you going to break the spell now that we're safely out of the building?" Matt asked.

"No," Missy said. "It will wear off eventually, probably by tomorrow. A guy like that, he deserves to be made to tell the truth a little more. Just imagine what he'll reveal to his wife tonight."

"I would hate to witness that."

MISSY WANTED to visit Myron and use the truth spell on him, too, so he would divulge where Ophelia, AKA Ruth, was. She was certain her mother wouldn't be home, because she knew Missy could find her there. The lawyer probably had her in a safe place while she cast the doomsday spell to wipe out all the manatees. There would be very little time left to find and stop her.

But Myron wouldn't take her or Matt's calls. They would have to travel to Tallahassee and confront him in person. It would take too long to drive there, so they hopped on the first flight the following morning.

The day of the full moon.

Florida's state capital was a city of contrasts. Part college town, part down-home Southern city, and part theme park for the con men and scoundrels that gravitate to state government.

Missy and Matt rented a car at the airport and drove straight to Myron's office on Duval Street.

It was a fairly modern but nondescript office building. The directory in the lobby was filled with names of law firms and suspicious sounding organizations that probably funneled dark money contributions, names like "Americans for the American Way of Being American." Myron's office was on the fifth floor. But the outer office door was locked. No one was in yet. They had no choice but to wait until someone showed up.

"What if he won't see us?" Matt asked.

"He'll have to walk past us. We won't let him blow us off."

"I can be as persistent as any reporter, but if the guy doesn't want to tell us where the sorceress is—and he surely won't—we can't make him talk. Unless we threaten to harm him, which is a felony. Or, a certain witch uses her magick on him to keep him from going into his office and locking us out."

"I have a binding spell to constrain him," Missy said. "Then I'll use the truth-telling spell. I'm running a little short on the powder, though. I've been using it so much lately. I can't afford to sprinkle any on the floor by accident."

They stood in the hall waiting. Every time the elevator door opened, they looked up expectantly, but no one came to Myron's office. Missy tried to fight back the growing anxiety that somewhere her mother was going to unleash some sort of magic that would kill all the manatees.

Tonight was the full moon, the most opportune time to generate massive amounts of power for a big spell. And the scary fact was, her mother didn't have to wait until night when the moon was visible. Because it was visible on the other side of the planet right now.

The stench of rotten eggs filled her nostrils. She frowned at Matt.

"Hey, it wasn't me," he said. "I thought it was you. At least I was polite enough not to frown at you."

Missy placed her palms on the office doorway.

"Oh, my. I feel dark energy inside. There's black magic being generated for sure. I think my mother is in there right now."

"Can you unlock the door?" Matt asked. "Sorry, I know that's a sensitive topic."

Everyone thinks witches can just wave a hand and unlock doors, but Missy struggled with it. She used various spells, or her telekinesis, or both in combination. She was getting better at it, but unlocking something was never guaranteed.

This door had a pad for card keys to unlock it electronically. That was a good thing. This more advanced kind of lock was actually easier for her magick to open.

She took the power charm from her pocket, cupped it in both hands, and concentrated her inner energies. Instead of using power from the charm, she added her power to it. Reciting a short verse in Old English, she held the power charm up to the pad like a card key. She couldn't match the magnetic code, but she instead sent a surge of electromagnetic power strong enough to shift the bolt.

The lock clicked. She pulled the door open and walked into a small reception area. Short hallways lined with offices extended to her right and left. Matt followed her and shut the door behind him.

Chanting came from a room on the left-hand hallway. It was a hoarse female voice, manic and sputtering, voicing an ancient foreign tongue that sent chills down Missy's spine.

She ran down the hallway, armed with nothing but her magick and the Red Dragon talisman she had brought from home, just in case she needed it.

As waves of evil magic emanated from down the hall, she was certain she'd need it.

A doorway labeled "Conference Room" glowed, as if a terrible fire raged behind it. No one else would see that glow except a trained witch with innate paranormal abilities.

The glow meant going into this room would be like walking into a nuclear reactor.

But she had to do it, even if the intensity of the black magic in there damaged her.

The door was locked, of course, but this was a simple lock and she defeated it with her telekinesis alone. The door opened inward.

Her mother knelt on a long table. It hovered at least a foot above the floor. The air was shimmering, and looking at her mother was like viewing her behind a waterfall.

A black object the size and shape of a human heart lay on the table in front of her mother. She held a dove above the heart. Blood poured from the bird onto the heart, hissing and turning to vapor as it landed on the stone.

Her mother cackled when she saw Missy.

"You're too late, girlie. This spell is ready to go."

But she continued to chant.

She's lying, Missy thought. It's not complete quite yet.

Missy pushed toward the table. It was like walking into a hurricane wind. Her mother wasn't looking at her now. She stared at the ceiling, the muscles in her neck bulging, spittle spraying from her mouth as she chanted.

Acting only on impulse, Missy swung her arm and knocked the black heart from the table. It flew across the room and smashed the glass covering a picture of a troll-like man shaking hands with a recent president. The picture fell to the floor.

"Oh, you think that's going to make a difference? You're a fool," her mother said.

At least it threw her mother off balance for a moment.

Giving Missy time to grasp the Red Dragon and shout the words of a negation spell as her body throbbed with the talisman's power.

But a tremendous force hit her and knocked her off her feet. The Red Dragon escaped her hand and landed somewhere behind her.

Her mother cackled.

"Now I'm going to finally get rid of you for good, girlie."

22

YOU ARE SO DEAD

Missy scrambled on her hands and knees to reach the metal talisman which had rolled to a stop underneath a chair against the wall. She had worried about bringing it with her, because she didn't want her mother to know she had the legendary artifact. She couldn't allow any possibility of her mother stealing it from her. And now look what happened.

Her forward motion ceased. A force held her legs in a vice-like grip and pulled her backwards toward the conference table.

"Come here, you little brat," her mother said. "And take your medicine."

Missy focused on the wall receding from her. A dry-erase board was mounted on it, covered in words scrawled with a marker:

"Our four pillars: 1. Greed 2. Ruthlessness 3. Dishonesty 4. Lust for Power."

How unoriginal, Missy thought. It sounded like any lawyer or client.

Refocusing her attention on the wall, she cast a snare spell, attempting to attach herself to the wall like the strands of a spider's web.

The invisible ropes of power adhered to the wall and tightened. She stopped sliding toward her mother.

Now what?

Whatever force her mother was using pulled harder. Sharp pain flared in Missy's knees and hips as if her legs were about to be pulled from her like chicken bones.

She needed to change the balance of power here fast. Her advantage was her mother needed to remain within her magic circle and inverted pentagram on the table. And her mother was in the middle of creating the massive die-off spell. If she put all her attention into killing Missy, her spell would crumble apart and might not be able to be replicated.

Missy's disadvantage was the truth that her mother's black magic was a far more powerful offensive weapon than any spell Missy had. It was a disadvantage that could prove fatal.

Even her best defense, her protection spell, was useless against her mother. Missy turned it off to save her energy for something else.

One strand of her binding spell broke free from the wall under the unrelenting force, pulling Missy toward her mother. Then another one detached.

Missy turned her head back to look at her mother. The sorceress wasn't paying full attention to killing her. She had somehow returned the black heart to her magic circle and was still trying to complete the die-off spell. It was like a cook busy sautéing a main dish in the skillet while keeping an eye on the vegetables simmering in another pot on the back burner. Missy was the vegetables. She felt like overcooked cabbage and twice as nasty.

It was time to gamble.

Missy released her binding spell from the wall and instantly snapped backwards like a retractable power cord into a vacuum cleaner. The back of her shoulders hit the edge of the conference table with a flash of pain.

Her mother cackled with glee and grabbed Missy's throat with one hand. And that hand was stronger than it ought to be on a woman of her mother's age. It squeezed Missy's esophagus, constricting her windpipe. She struggled to breathe, spots swimming across her vision.

Maybe this gamble wasn't such a good idea. But Missy went ahead with it. She reached up across the table and grabbed the black heart.

Her reaching hand removing the heart violated the magic circle. Her mother's spell paused again.

The evil sorceress bellowed with rage. Missy sensed the energies swirling in the air from the disturbed equilibrium and her mother's attempt to stabilize the complex tapestry of magic she had woven before it came apart. Magic as powerful as that took hours of work and gigantic reserves of energy to build, not to mention whatever evil powers had been added to it. If it all came apart, there was no guarantee her mother had the strength to rebuild it again.

The grip on Missy's throat loosened slightly, allowing her to gulp air before she passed out.

The black heart was hot, almost to the point of burning Missy's hands. It was as hard as a rock. It felt as if it had been carved from obsidian, but Missy knew better. It was an unworldly material created from evil and toxic human emotions like hate and anger. She tried to crush it in her hands, but it was too solid.

Simply holding it was likely unsafe for her, as if it were plutonium.

"Give that back to me!"

Her mother released Missy's throat and reached for the heart. Missy was still held against the table by whatever spell had dragged her here, but she could extend her arms and keep the heart from her mother's reach.

Her mother swiveled around on the tabletop to face Missy and grabbed her neck with both hands. Her grip was like a python's, blocking Missy's air as well as the blood going to her brain. Missy moved with the strength of someone about to die.

She swung her arms backwards over her head and smashed her mother in the head with the rock-like heart.

Her mother yelped. The hands on her neck loosened slightly.

Missy pounded her mother's skull again. And again.

Her mother released her neck and grabbed Missy's wrists and tried to pry them apart. Missy couldn't believe how strong her mother was, especially after getting brained with the heart. Evil, it seemed, was a great energy booster.

Missy struggled to get another blow in, but her mother wouldn't allow it.

So, still holding the heart, Missy suddenly flung her arms forward, over her body.

Her mother, still holding Missy's wrists, slid across the glossy surface of the table and slipped off, landing next to her daughter.

She was out of the magic circle. The spell was broken. But not gone. It was too powerful and complex to dissipate quickly. Its energies still hung in the air, slowly coming apart, but not yet beyond repairing.

"You brat!" her mother screamed.

She scrambled to her feet and lunged.

Missy slammed the heart into her face. Something crunched.

"You broke my nose, you turd!"

Blood streamed from her mother's nose and from a cut above her eyes.

The spell that was holding Missy's back against the table edge weakened. Missy broke away and ran across the room to the chair against the wall.

She reached beneath it and grabbed the Red Dragon, its warm metal pulsing with power, feeling good in her left hand.

Her mother came at her again.

Missy quickly cast a binding spell, making her mother freeze in place as if she were wrapped in ropes. Missy didn't need the talisman to cast this spell, but it made the spell dozens of times stronger.

But she did need the talisman for what came next: a nullification spell to undo the die-off spell her mother had conjured.

While her mother screamed in anger and frustration, Missy methodically disassembled the complex spell, pulling it apart thread by thread, loosening knots, dissolving the magic welds.

The amount of energy the dissolving spell released was staggering. So much evil had gone into making this, enough to cover the entire state of Florida and kill each and every manatee.

It was a nuclear bomb of evil magic. And Missy faced the radiation exposure as she destroyed the deadly weapon.

The black heart in her right hand quickly cooled to room temperature. Then it crumbled into dust that fell between her fingers onto the floor.

"You'll pay for that," her mother said. "I still have time to rebuild the spell before the full moon wanes. After I kill you."

"You didn't build that spell on your own."

"I had a little help. From a friend."

"From a demon, I'm sure."

"Some demons make good friends. But it usually doesn't end well for the human."

"I don't know what to do with you," Missy said. "You need to be behind bars for the rest of your life."

"You can't convict me on witchcraft. We're not in Salem during the witch-hunting hysteria."

"I'll find a way. There are a lot of dead manatees because of you."

"I was only doing a job for a client."

"And one day I'm going to prove you killed my father."

"The state listed his cause of death as a freak dishwasher accident. They'll never believe a demon did it. And you'll never prove that I summoned the demon. You'll never put me in prison."

"I should kill you, then."

Her mother cackled. Then broke into a phlegmy cough.

"You don't have it in you to kill me. Now, release me from your spell. I need a cigarette."

"No. You're staying bound until the full moon passes."

"You really think I can't get out of your stupid binding spell? I was asking you nicely, to save me the trouble."

Missy didn't know if black magic had its equivalent of her nullification spell. In her eyes, black magic was a crude form of magic and relied too heavily on substances such as blood and grave dirt, as well as on demons and other entities, to do the heavy lifting, as opposed to the organic approach of her earth magick.

While she was thinking snobby thoughts about black magic, her mother hummed loudly in an annoying nasal tone.

Then she raised her arms and walked toward Missy.

So much for the superiority of her earth magick.

Her mother walked up to her and slapped her in the face. Missy squared her shoulders in defiance. Then kicked her mother in the knee, causing her to howl in pain.

Was this really how two magicians on opposite sides of the moral spectrum were going to battle it out?

No, it wasn't.

Her mother took a crouching stance with her flattened palms out, as if she were a martial arts fighter.

Lightning flew from her fingertips, and Missy bounced backwards, hitting the wall and convulsing from the electric shock. The smell of burnt clothing and hair was in the air.

Missy quickly cast a protection spell, though she knew it wouldn't be sufficient to stop her mother.

And it didn't.

The lightning bolts zapped her again. She fell to the floor engulfed in spasms.

Her mother stood over her, smiling in impending victory.

"I was right to give you up as an infant. You're too human, too weak. You have these stupid emotions of empathy and wanting to do what's right. Those are the symptoms of a loser. You can't be successful in this world if you care about other people. That's why you're a low-rent nurse giving enemas to vampires and werewolves."

Missy, totally vulnerable on the floor, looked up at her mother and said, "You gave birth to me. How can you hate me like this? You don't even know me. You missed my entire life."

"I gave birth to you just like a fish spawns minnows. Procreating doesn't mean love."

"Are you capable of love?"

Strangely, that caught her mother off guard. She cocked her head and thought about it.

"When I was a child, I loved my parents. When I first married your father, I loved him. But it didn't last. Love only means disappointment and hurt feelings. It's so much better not to love. It's so much better to hate. Hate is even more powerful than love."

"No, it's not," Missy said.

"Yes, it is. As you're about to find out."

An unseen force yanked Missy into the air until she crashed into the ceiling tiles. She remained suspended in the air horizontally.

"You're going to throw yourself through a window and get splattered on Duval Street. An obvious death by suicide. No one's fault but yours, the poor little girl who claimed she didn't have parental love."

"I did have love. My adoptive parents loved me unlike the mother of my blood."

"Spare me the histrionics," her birth mother said, as she used her magic to maneuver Missy across the ceiling and out into the hallway, like guiding a blimp with a line from the ground.

"You are so dead," her birth mother said.

She guided Missy to the office next door, which had a large plate-glass window overlooking Duval Street. Missy was rotated until her head faced the window.

"Again, nothing can tie me to your death," her birth mother said. "No magic involved. You just took a dive out the window by your own free will."

Missy felt the surge of energy crackling in the air, and her floating body quivered as the energy coalesced around it.

"Goodbye, my daughter."

23

PERVERTED MAGIC

Missy floated in the air horizontally, facing the
ground. Her head pointed toward a large window
overlooking Duval Street. She was partly para-
lyzed, only able to move her limbs slightly. She'd never felt this
helpless in her life.

A life that was about to end any moment now.

She felt the dark energy build up around her as her mother
waved her arms and chanted in an unknown tongue, building
up the kinetic energy that would rocket Missy forward to
smash through the window and plunge five stories to the street
below. Her mother had to build a substantial force to do it,
because office windows were very durable nowadays. That
meant breaking through the glass with her head would be
enough to kill Missy before she hit the ground.

Missy desperately worked on a nullification spell to
counter the black magic. She couldn't use the extra energy she
normally received from her power charm. And it was difficult
for her to disassemble a black-magic spell, because it was

based on very different parameters than her own earth magick.

She was running out of time.

Her mother stepped back from the window for safety. Her chanting reached a climax.

The black magic crackled upon Missy's skin.

Her mother raised her arms, poised to fling them toward the window as she screamed the last word of her chant.

And Matt burst into the office. He leaped and tackled Missy's mother just as her arms began their downward arc. The two bodies crashed upon the floor, knocking chairs over, before sliding to a halt.

Matt wrestled with the sorceress until he got her into a secure hold.

"I was on the wrestling team in school," he said panting, "and this old lady is stronger than a lot my opponents."

"Let go of me, you criminal!" his current opponent screamed.

"Don't let her arms move," Missy told him.

Missy still hovered six feet in the air, semi-paralyzed. The spell hadn't broken. It was still intact, as if set on pause. The only reason her mother wasn't using her magic to free herself was all of it was still engaged in the spell affecting Missy.

"So where the heck have you been all this time?" Missy asked Matt. "You wait to show up until two seconds before I'm launched though the window?"

"I didn't think I could help you to do your witch stuff. So I snooped around and found Myron Hickey's office. He has the unfortunate habit of printing out some of his emails and he didn't spend any effort hiding them. So I took pictures of them. There was also an addendum to a contract with a 'sorcery contractor' with additional fees for 'eradication services.' Pretty incriminating, in my opinion, if we can find a way to explain their plot without using magical terms."

"Good luck with that," her mother said.

Missy needed some help from her power charm to break her mother's spell. But her arm was too immobilized to reach into her pocket to get it. And Matt couldn't help her without letting go of her mother.

Her binding spell had been only temporarily effective with the sorceress. She decided to try something else.

She redirected the energies she had been gathering for the nullification spell. Then she chanted the invocation in Latin.

Her mother went limp beneath Matt.

"What happened?" he asked.

"My sleeping spell."

Her mother began snoring like a buzz saw.

"As you can tell, I can't move my limbs. I need you to get my power charm from my left pocket and put it in my left hand. Just keep an eye on her to make sure she doesn't wake up."

Matt climbed off her mother and reached up toward Missy.

"And don't get any naughty ideas," she warned him.

He reached into the left pocket of her jeans. The intimacy of his hand sliding over her upper thigh sent electricity through her that had nothing to do with black magic.

He removed the charm, a small cloth sack filled with herbs, powders, and rare stones all infused with her magick. He placed it in her left hand and curled her fingers around it.

"Thank you," she said, her face still flushed from his hand in her pocket. "Keep an eye on my mother."

Now, with the boost from her power charm, she could complete the nullification spell. She discovered the black-magic spell that was meant to kill her drew most of its power from the souls of the damned in Hell and a little natural energy from a tropical depression forming in the Gulf of Mexico. Missy disassembled it in about ten minutes.

She dropped to the ground, almost hitting her head on the desk.

"Are you okay?" Matt asked.

Missy got to her feet. "Only my dignity was hurt. Keep her arms secure, just in case. I'll be right back."

She went down the hall and returned to the conference room. The Red Dragon talisman still lay beneath the chair along the wall. She felt so much better having it in her pocket again.

She had to create some sort of spell that would prevent her mother from recreating the die-off spell against the manatees. But she needed a little advice.

"Don Mateo," she said, "please come to me."

The seventeenth century Spanish wizard's ghost was bound to her, but that didn't mean he always showed up when requested.

"Don Mateo, I humbly request your assistance,"

She waited. No ghost. She grasped the Red Dragon in her left hand.

"Don Mateo, by the power of the Red Dragon, I command you to appear before me."

And there he was, sitting in his breeches and doublet in a chair at the head of the conference table. A wide-brimmed hat with a feather in its band sat on his head.

"What can I do for you, my lady?"

"Please help me create a spell. I need to prevent my mother from using black magic to create a massive die-off of the manatees in Florida. The spell will have to work whenever there's a full moon. And she'll be summoning a demon to give her the power to cast it. I was able to use a nullification spell to stop her today, but I can't watch her every minute of every full moon to stop her next time she tries it."

"Egad, that's a difficult one. Demons are so unpredictable. I learned that the hard way."

In a parlor trick to impress a friend, Don Mateo had accidentally summoned a demon. It did not go well. He had to continue his wizard career as a ghost.

"My advice," he continued, "would be to not attempt nullifying her spell. Rather, we'll create a way to pervert it. A spell that attaches to her and activates whenever she creates this die-off spell. It then turns her spell into something else, something harmless."

"That's a wonderful idea," Missy said.

"It is, if I don't say so myself. Now, tell me the details of how her spell was constructed, that you learned when you nullified it. Then we'll create our counteracting spell."

Missy explained to him, as best she could, the complex tapestry of black magic that her mother had woven, and Missy had meticulously picked apart. She described how the spell's power came from the black heart. She guessed the heart had been created by the demon as a manifestation of the evil in humans' hearts.

"Quite an impressive sorceress your mother is," said Don Mateo.

"Whatever. First and foremost, she's evil. That's all that matters."

"Since this spell is based on evil intentions, let's devise a way to turn them on their head."

Missy used a note-taking app on her phone to write down the ideas she and the wizard's ghost came up with. With some thorough editing, she eventually had the outlines of a spell that just might work. You could call it a recipe for the spell creating.

"Are you ready to begin?" Don Mateo asked.

"I am. I sure hope this works."

She returned to the office where her mother still snored on the floor and Matt stood guard. Don Mateo floated along with her, though he was not visible to Matt.

"I have to ask you to step into the hall," she said to Matt. "There's going to be some dangerous magick in this room."

He jumped out and closed the door.

Missy found a marker on the desk and drew a magick circle on the carpet and around herself and the prone body of her mother. She would have to do without candles today, but that was okay.

As she always did, she began by clearing her mind and gathering up her internal energies, and then those from the earth and the other elements. Being on the fifth floor of a modern office building made that a bit tricky, but she linked to the energies, nevertheless. Then she held the Red Dragon talisman in both hands. She never ceased to be amazed by the power it held and how it surged through her body and mind.

It took several minutes to construct the spell and then recite the invocation that Don Mateo had written in Latin for her. She read it from her smartphone screen, which she placed far enough outside the magick circle that the magick wouldn't fry it.

The last step was to send the spell into her mother. She did this with pleasure, watching her mother jump as if shocked with defibrillator paddles as the powerful magick flowed into her. As the magick traveled from Missy into her mother, she felt drained and exhausted. That was a sign that the transfer had worked.

At last, the spell was completed. Missy stepped out of the circle.

Her mother still slept. Missy realized the reason her sleeping spell remained working, while her binding spell hadn't, was because her mother couldn't undo it, since she was asleep. She could have prevented the sleeping spell from beginning, but Missy had cast it before her mother had realized what was going on.

She cast an add-on to the spell which would cause it to last a little longer before it wore off, until she and Matt were safely away from the city.

"I hope the counteracting spell works," Missy said. "But how will we know?"

"We might not know," Don Mateo said. "It depends on what the perverted spell does. But you will know for sure we were successful if the manatees survive."

Missy thanked the wizard and released him. Then she and Matt returned to the airport, where they moved their return flight to the next scheduled departure.

"I have to say that it's hard to imagine a sweet person like you coming from a mother like that," Matt said.

"I know. I'm so glad she didn't raise me. But I worry sometimes about the genes I inherited from her. I think I got my paranormal abilities from my father. Who knows what I got from this wretched creature."

"Your stubbornness?"

Missy gave him a sideways look. "If so, I hope that's the only thing I got from her."

WHEN SHE RETURNED HOME, and in the coming days, Missy repeatedly checked the local news on TV and internet news sites for any word of a manatee die-off. To her great relief, there was nothing. Perhaps her mother hadn't been able to cast her spell before the full moon waned. Or she did cast the spell, but it didn't work.

Then she came across signs that her mother did, indeed, cast her spell, but it had the opposite effect than what was intended.

Missy saw headlines about a recent census finding growth in the manatee population. Then others describing the mating season starting now, months before it normally did.

There were even stranger tales. Groups of manatees seemed to be acting in coordination to ram speeding boats from the side, causing them to lose control and crash into seawalls and other boats. Manatees were supposed to be gentle and slow-moving, but these reports described them as aggressive with dolphin-like speed.

In a stretch of the Intracoastal Waterway north of Crab County, a gigantic herd of sea cows actually formed a blockade across the waterway. Some were injured by speeding boats, but most of the boats that attempted to pass were knocked out of control or made to capsize. Soon, they entirely shut down boat traffic for two days.

Mothers for Manatees brought heads of lettuce and fresh water for the manatees in the blockade so they could stay on the line.

On the second day, a boatload of thugs fired weapons at the creatures. They were promptly arrested and vilified in the news.

Mothers for Manatees did a massive public relations campaign, celebrating the courage of the manatees. It increased awareness of the animals' endangered status and the ways to protect them. And it brought in millions of dollars in contributions.

In fact, the organization's war chest expanded so greatly

that a high-powered lawyer named Myron Hickey approached them and offered his services to lobby government for stricter manatee protections. But immediately afterward, news emerged about a federal investigation into alleged lawbreaking by his firm. He took the next flight to Brazil and disappeared.

The manatees had none other than Ophelia Lawthorne, AKA Ruth Bent, and her perverted spell, to thank for their improved lives. The evil sorceress must be banging her head on the table right now, Missy thought.

Myron's anti-manatee clients were undoubtedly upset as well. Bob Pistaulover found himself under federal investigation. Missy wasn't confident he'd end up being indicted, but she was pleased to see stories in the news (many of which were written by Matt), about allegations the CEO had been trying to harm manatees. Barbarian Boat Works' sales went down the toilet.

Missy was ecstatic to see that evil was punished, even if in weird, indirect ways.

24

M 4 M

"You didn't bring me any batteries," Sylvia said when Maria returned home.

"Sorry. I forgot."

Sylvia was draped across the sofa in the living room, watching TV. A young Caucasian man in a tight T-shirt with puncture wounds in his neck lay unconscious on the floor next to her. A used syringe rested in his hand.

Maria was disgusted by the sight.

"How'd it go?" Sylvia asked.

"What do you mean?"

"The witch. You said you were going to kill the witch."

"I messed up again," Maria said, sitting in an armchair with stuffing protruding from a tear in the fabric. "A bunch of geezer vampires stopped me. It turns out this witch is also their home health nurse. And these vampires are so old they really do need a nurse."

"Come sit next to me," Sylvia said, patting the sofa cushion.

Maria ignored her. "This fifteen-hundred-year-old vampire

told me their retirement community was trying to get all the vampires of Jellyfish Beach to cooperate for mutual protection."

"Enrico said a few of them came by here the other night asking the same thing. He wouldn't commit to them. He wants his hive to be independent."

"What happens if we get in trouble?"

"You say 'we' as if you're a member of the hive. You need to behave like you want to be one of us," Sylvia said with a taunting smile. She patted the sofa cushion again.

"My maker was part of a clan that tried to conquer all the vampires around here. A small hive like yours couldn't fight back against something like that."

"Yeah, but how likely is it that something like that would happen again?"

"And the drugs," Maria said. "The police could arrest you all or stake you, even."

"Humans can't harm us. Their guns can't kill us and there's no way they could be fast and strong enough to stake one of us."

"If there were enough of them, they could."

Sylvia laughed dismissively and returned her attention to the TV.

Maria glanced around the room. This house was depressing. The once-elegant historical home had been allowed to deteriorate and there was no excuse for it. The hive didn't use the drugs they lured their victims with, but they acted like a bunch of addicts too lazy and strung out to care about anything. They were decadent and cynical and cared about nothing other than feeding and sensual pleasures. Maria couldn't imagine spending eternity that way.

"It's getting near dawn," Sylvia said languidly. "Come join me in bed, darling."

Maria stood and moved toward the door.

"I feel bad that I forgot your batteries. I'm going to run out really quick to get them. I'll be right back."

AGNES WAS surprised when her doorbell rang shortly before dawn. She opened the door to find Maria standing there.

"Is your offer still good for me to stay here?" the young woman asked.

"Of course," Agnes replied.

"Are pets allowed?"

"Two pets under forty pounds each. But very few vampires here have pets."

"So a thousand-pound vampire cave bear wouldn't be allowed?"

"We'll discuss it later, dear," Agnes said. "I'm the president of the HOA. Exceptions can always be made."

BOB PISTAULOVER NEEDED TO UNWIND. He was tired of being unfairly harassed by the FBI, FWC, EPA, and a bunch of other acronyms. He was tempted to call it a witch hunt, but given his involvement with an actual witch, he decided not to.

It was the perfect time to have a sunset pool party at his $46-million oceanside mansion.

His sixth wife, Greta, invited all her society cronies. He invited his top executives and their spouses, which meant they were mandated to attend. Several politicians managed to invite themselves. The caterers served caviar and champagne poolside. This year's Grammy-winning singer, Pistaulover always forgot her name, performed. The crowd filled the expansive lanai alongside the Olympic-sized pool and gazed at the moon reflecting off the ocean. It was a great evening to be rich.

Though it was meant to be a casual pool party, no one was wearing a bathing suit or was in the pool, which disappointed Bob. There were enough plastic surgery patients here to support the entire industry, and he really wanted to see some skimpy bikinis. So he broke the ice and changed into his bathing trunks. He walked along the pool toward the diving board, completely unembarrassed by his bloated gut hanging over his trunks to the point he couldn't even see his feet.

He planned to do a cannonball dive from the board, which would splash half the guests and really get the party rolling.

MOTHERS FOR MANATEES attacked on two fronts in a pincer movement. One boat arrived via the Intracoastal. Pistaulover's waterfront estate included an additional parcel of land across the street, giving him access to the Intracoastal as well as the ocean. He had a large dock where he kept a ski boat and a giant, fuel-guzzling cabin cruiser he had custom-built to drive at high speeds in great luxury. It was named *The Beast*, but he affectionately nicknamed it "The Manatee Killer."

Within minutes, both boats were in flames. Mothers for Manatees, wearing black commando outfits, charged across the street to spray-paint slogans on the facade of Pistaulover's mansion and hoist a hundred-foot-long banner that read: "Save the sea cows from the human pigs! M4M."

The other M4M team had traveled along the coast and anchored just off the beach in front of the mansion. While the wealthy guests sipped champagne and gossiped, the raiders surfed on paddle boards from their mothership and landed on the beach. They worked quickly.

PISTAULOVER STOOD on the diving board. A few guests taunted him to jump in. He made jokes about doing a somersault dive as he bounced at the end of the board.

He abruptly stopped.

On the top of the sand dunes was a long banner supported by stakes in the sand. It said, "Save the manatees. Tax the pigs."

Do they mean farm pigs? he wondered. Pigs can't pay taxes. Or are they referring to people like him?

He stared in amazement as two people clad like Ninjas ran onto his property, right past a confused security guard. They didn't carry weapons. They seemed harmless, but what were they doing?

He soon found out. One of them, a big lumbering person who appeared to be a man beneath the mask, broke toward the pool. He ran onto the diving board, and there, in front of all his guests, punched Pistaulover in the mouth. Then he pulled down Pistaulover's bathing trunks. The man thudded away off the diving board and toward the beach.

A few guests laughed, thinking this was part of a planned comedy sketch.

Pistaulover's mind reeled as he relived the trauma of his childhood: his bathing suit falling off because of a manatee. The girls laughing at him.

Here he was, immensely rich and powerful, yet once again, being laughed at while his bathing suit was down around his ankles.

He jumped into the pool in shame, splashing his caviar-eating guests with pool water.

The parting gift of the M4M team? Clouds of tear gas and pepper spray released as they retreated to their paddle boards and made their escape.

As his guests coughed and choked in the fumes, at least Pistaulover wasn't the only person there with tears in his eyes.

Myron Hickey didn't get off as easily as Pistaulover. His body was found by the police in Rio de Janeiro in his hotel room. He had drowned with his head stuck in the toilet bowl. The toilet was filled with what the lab later identified as pumpkin-spice beer.

The bathroom mirror was tagged with "M4M" written in shaving cream. The detectives theorized that this was a new street gang they had never heard of. A gang truly to be feared.

The final target for retribution by Mothers for Manatees was a black-magic sorcerous named Ruth Bent. To this day, they have been unable to locate her.

But they remained vigilant, as ever, guarding the waterways of Florida.

SHIFTING FORTUNES

Once again, Missy arrived at the security gate for Barbarian Boat Works in a white rental van. The same middle-aged woman guard was there, with eyes glued to her tablet through thick glasses.

"UPSP," Missy said, holding up the same fake package she used last time.

The guard buzzed the gate open.

Missy followed the road around the parking lot and instead of approaching the office building, she followed the road to the factory. This time, however, she kept going past the gigantic building. She ignored the signs saying this was a restricted area and continued following the road, which was now unpaved. It was late in the afternoon, and it appeared that activity had wound down for the day.

She passed the outbuildings she had seen during her astral travel. Up ahead was the repair shop. Her heart skipped a beat. The giant boat wasn't there on its trailer. Hopefully, it was inside the shop, because she wouldn't be able to find it otherwise.

She parked and carried her fake package to the building. At one end was a large garage door which was open. Relief swept through her when she saw the boat perched atop wooden scaffolding. The hull had been repaired and painted, with the registration number removed. The sharp tang of varnish filled the air. Fortunately, no one was inside the building.

With no time to waste, she went inside. A step ladder stood on the right side of the boat. She took a piece of chalk from her pocket and drew a large circle on the concrete floor around the legs of the ladder with plenty of room to spare. Then she climbed the ladder. When she was high enough, she reached over and grasped the steering wheel in her left hand, hoping the blond man's psychic energy would be on it.

It was. She sensed it even before she cast the spell that would find where he lived, so she could send the police there to take the "person of interest" in for interrogation. After she and Matt had relayed the incriminating information they had about Pistaulover and his minions to the police, the murderer would be in hiding.

She grasped the power charm in her right hand and gathered her energies. While she and the ladder were within the magick circle she had drawn, she would soon find out if being eight feet above the circle would work. As the power amassed inside her, it appeared to be working.

It was time for the invocation. She recited the words from memory, the sharp consonants and long vowels of the long-dead language. Power flowed from the charm in her right hand, through her heart, and down along her left arm to the steering wheel.

Soon, the orb of the man's psychic energy would form.

"And what do you think you're doing?" The man's voice had a Russian accent.

She turned her head and looked down at the tall man with the wavy blond hair. His face was long and angular, expressionless. An ugly scar ran beneath his right eye. He regarded her like a bug to squish.

He looked like a psychopath, except for his blond mane. If a guy wanted to have hair like that, he needed to be wearing a tight-fitting sequined outfit that revealed a lot of chest hair and he needed to be holding an electric guitar. Otherwise, it was just silly.

Her spell's power faded as she scrambled to think of Plan B.

"You shouldn't be in here," the man said as he approached the ladder. "This is a very expensive boat. You wouldn't be a reporter, would you?"

"Just delivering a package for UPSP," Missy said. "This boat is awesome. I couldn't resist checking it out."

"In my mother country, we have ways of dealing with troublesome reporters. Permanent ways."

He raised the bottom of his shirt enough to show the butt of a handgun stuck in his pants. Standing at the base of the ladder, he grasped the side rails with both hands.

"It is very dangerous climbing tall ladders when you are not experienced," he said. "An accidental fall could be deadly. Tell me why you're here."

An electric jolt ran up her arm from her power charm.

"*Dormi!* she commanded, followed by an additional string of Latin.

The blond man took two unsteady steps backwards and rubbed his face with his hands. He shook his head as if his hair was wet.

Then he slowly collapsed upon the floor. His snoring echoed in the repair shop.

Her sleeping spell worked. But for extra insurance, she gathered her energies for another spell and recited an invocation in Old English. The blond man straightened out on the floor and went rigid, as if he had a seizure.

It wasn't a seizure. It was her binding spell. The man was now completely neutralized.

Still on the ladder, she called 911 and reported that a murder suspect wanted to turn himself in at the Barbarian Boat Works repair shop behind the factory.

Since she was trespassing, she decided it was best to leave the scene. She drove the rental van off the boat works property and parked on the side of the road close to the gate. When two patrol cars entered the property, she waited long enough for them to park at the repair shop and find the blond man. Then she nullified the two spells that had immobilized him.

It would be a very depressing way for him to wake up.

MISSY CHECKED the news religiously for mentions of manatee deaths, and they had become extremely rare. She didn't know how long the perverted version of her mother's spell would last, but apparently the manatees were still enjoying newly found speed and agility, not to mention aggressiveness. She hoped this latter characteristic would fade soon before there was a public backlash against the creatures for all the boats they forced to run aground.

The important fact was that they hadn't been wiped out, and her mother hadn't managed to do so with an alternate spell.

Seymour disappeared from her home more and more often.

He claimed to be going to the municipal swimming pool for exercise, but when he returned, he didn't smell of chlorine. Rather, he had the briny smell of an estuary's brackish water. In other words, he'd been swimming in the Intracoastal Waterway.

Seymour was shifting into a manatee on his own again, she was certain. His sea-cow heritage was calling him.

"Seymour, I think you've gotten all the revenge you can get," she told him gently one morning over tea and romaine heads. "Without committing murder, that is. Though you did push the legal boundaries by trespassing on Pistaulover's property with the Mothers for Manatees and assaulting him."

Seymour smiled at the memory.

"You've done all you can do to avenge Lubblubb," Missy said.

"What about the lawyer? And his other clients that paid to kill manatees?"

"Myron Hickey fled the country and was murdered in Rio. His clients are under investigation. And Mothers for Manatees won't let them go unpunished."

"And the sorceress. Your mother. She's still out there. She can try a new, deadlier, spell."

"First of all, she won't do anything if she isn't paid for it. No one is paying her anymore."

Seymour nodded.

"And secondly," she continued, "I have my own agenda. My mother is going to suffer for this. And I'm going to make sure she sees justice for having my father killed. It could take me a long time. But I'm going to be on her butt like a nasty rash, and she won't get rid of me until I'm satisfied. So you can cross her off the list of people you need to punish."

Seymour nodded. His face had a stricken look.

"If you want to return to manatee life, you can do it whenever you're ready."

"Are you trying to get rid of me?" he asked.

I sure as heck am, she thought.

"Not at all," she said in her sweetest voice. "You've been a good friend. In your kind of weird way."

"There were certain times it felt good to be a human again. Things I missed when I was a manatee. Like television. Potato chips. Pretty women."

His little piggy eyes looked pleadingly at her.

"You found love among the manatees before," she said. "You'll do it again."

He looked away, into the distance.

"To tell the truth, the human world is too stressful for me. Too much stuff cluttering your life. Too many things to worry about. Deadlines and late fees and retirement savings. Ugh. I just can't stand it. I also wasn't so good at socializing. Never had a lot of friends. It was so much easier as a manatee. No one had hidden agendas. I had no problem fitting in, as long as there weren't any grumpy old bulls in the herd. I never felt alone as a manatee."

"Whenever you're ready to leave, just let me know."

HE DIDN'T LET her know. Two days later, when she returned from a shift just before dawn, she found a note laying on the kitchen counter. The handwriting was atrocious, which was to be expected from a human who hadn't written anything for decades. The note merely said:

"Thank you, Missy, for your help and hospitality. Your

goodness and grace will endear you to all. I will never forget you. And your hot body. Love, Seymour."

Once, when she was kayaking several months later, a hiss of breath told her a manatee had surfaced nearby. The creature had tufts of hair that resembled eyebrows, and something seemed familiar about its face.

"Seymour?" she asked aloud.

The huge sea cow swam right beside her kayak. It was almost as long as the boat.

It tapped the hull twice with its flipper. Then dove beneath the surface.

"Stay well, my friend," Missy said.

THE END

WHAT'S NEXT

GET A FREE E-BOOK

Sign up for my newsletter and get *Hangry as Hell*, a Freaky Florida novella, for free. If you join, you'll get news, fun articles, and lots of free book promotions, delivered only a couple of times a month. No spam at all, and you can unsubscribe at any time.

Sign up at wardparker.com

CHECK OUT MY NEW SERIES: The Memory Guild midlife paranormal mysteries.

Starting anew at midlife, with two marriages behind her, innkeeper Darla Chesswick returns to her hometown. There has always been a bit of the paranormal in her family, but now she discovers she has psychometry, too—the ability to read people's memories by touching objects they have touched. And in San Marcos, founded by the Spanish in Florida five centuries ago, there are plenty of memories. Many of them deadly. Learn more at wardparker.com

ENJOY THIS BOOK? PLEASE LEAVE A REVIEW

In the Amazon universe, the number of reviews readers leave can make or break a book. I would be very grateful if you could spend just a few minutes and write a fair and honest review. It can be as short or long as you wish. Just go to amazon.com, search for "dirty old manatee ward parker," and click the link for leaving reviews. Thanks!

COMING NEXT IN FREAKY FLORIDA

Book 7, *Gazillions of Reptilians*

Are lizards the wizards of doom?

Midlife witch Missy Mindle is busy enough as a home health nurse for elderly vampires and werewolves in Jellyfish Beach, Florida. But now she needs to solve a murder, too. Who or what killed Marvin Nutley, her vampire patient found incinerated on his oceanfront balcony?

Marvin believed in the Reptilian Conspiracy: that Lizard People are taking over the planet. He claimed to have a video showing a human turning into a dragon. He also claimed he shot said dragon. And now there's the threat of all-out war between vampires and dragons, and between humans and every reptile with teeth. To prevent it, Missy needs to find out if Marvin was killed by cold-blooded reptiles or a hot-headed vampire.

Find *Gazillions of Reptilians* on Amazon or wardparker.com

OTHER BOOKS IN FREAKY FLORIDA

Have you read Book 1, *Snowbirds of Prey*?

Retirement is deadly.

Centuries-old vampires who play pickleball. Aging werewolves who surf naked beneath the full moon. To survive, they must keep their identities secret, but all the dead humans popping up may spell their doom. Can Missy Mindle, midlife amateur witch, save them?

Get *Snowbirds of Prey* on Amazon or wardparker.com

Or Book 2, ***Invasive Species?***
Gators. Pythons. Iguanas.
Dragons?
Why not? It's Florida.
Missy, midlife amateur witch and nurse to elderly supernaturals, has two problems. First, she found a young, injured dragon in the Everglades with a price on its head. Second, her vampire patient Schwartz has disappeared after getting caught by Customs with werewolf blood. (It's like Viagra for vampires. Don't ask.)

Order *Invasive Species* today from Amazon or wardparker.com

Or Book 3, ***Fate Is a Witch?***
Missy Mindle has two mysteries to solve. First, who is making a series of dangerous magick attacks against her that appear to be tests of her growing witchy abilities? And who is stealing corpses from funeral homes in Jellyfish Beach? When an embalmer is murdered, one of Missy's patients, a werewolf, is arrested. Can she exonerate him? Oh, and don't forget the hordes of ghouls and Hemingway lookalikes. Who will stop them?

Get *Fate Is a Witch* from Amazon or wardparker.com

Or Book 4, ***Gnome Coming?***
They're coming for you.
Can you really blame garden gnomes for having a grudge? They're displayed as kitschy jokes, wounded by weed whackers,

peed on by dogs. After midlife witch Missy Mindle seriously bungles a spell, gnomes throughout Jellyfish Beach, Florida, are becoming possessed by an evil force and are exacting retribution. Missy has to undo the fast-spreading spell and stop the surge of "accidental" human deaths. The problem is, her regular job is home-health nurse for elderly supernaturals, and she also has to help solve the murder of one of her werewolf patients. Like the gnomes, the Werewolf Women's Club is out for revenge.

And something is coming for her, too.

Order *Gnome Coming* from Amazon or wardparker.com

Or Book 5, *Going Batty?*

A vampire tale even a caveman would love.

The retired vampires at Squid Tower in Jellyfish Beach, Florida, have it good. Until some ancient vampires show up. These strange bloodsuckers can turn into bats, unlike modern vampires. And they're also a bunch of Neanderthals. No, really. Not all Neanderthals went extinct. Some went undead. And now they want to rule all the vampires of Florida.

Missy Mindle, midlife witch and nurse to elderly supernaturals, uses her magick to help her vampire patients fight back. But when the Neanderthals start taking vampire hostages, and kidnap the daughter of Missy's cousin, get ready for a conflict of prehistoric proportions.

Find Going Batty on Amazon or wardparker.com

ABOUT THE AUTHOR

Ward is a Florida native and author of the Freaky Florida series, a romp through the Sunshine State with witches, vampires, werewolves, dragons, and other bizarre, mythical creatures such as #FloridaMan. His newest series is the Memory Guild midlife paranormal mysteries. He also pens the Zeke Adams Series of Florida-noir mysteries and The Teratologist Series of historical supernatural thrillers. Connect with him on social media: Twitter (@wardparker), Facebook (wardparkerauthor), BookBub, Goodreads, or wardparker.com

ALSO BY WARD PARKER

The Zeke Adams Florida-noir mystery series. You can buy *Pariah* and *Fur* on Amazon or wardparker.com

The Teratologist series of historical paranormal thrillers. Buy the first novel on Amazon or wardparker.com

"Gods and Reptiles," a Lovecraftian short story. Buy it on Amazon or wardparker.com

"The Power Doctor," a historical witchcraft short story. Get it on Amazon or wardparker.com